JEZERO CITY

COLONY FOUR MARS

GERALD M. KILBY

OUTER PLANET
MEDIA

Published by GMK, 2017

Copyright © 2017 by Gerald M. Kilby All rights reserved.

No part of this book may be reproduced, scanned, or distributed in any printed, or electronic form without express written permission.

Please do not participate in, or encourage piracy of copyrighted materials in violation of the author's rights. Purchase only authorized editions. This is a work of fiction. Names, characters, and incidents are either the product of the author's imagination or are used fictitiously. Any resemblance to actual persons, living or dead, businesses, companies or events is entirely coincidental.

This book has been edited for US English.
Version us1.1

For notifications on upcoming books, and access to my FREE starter library, please join my Readers Group at www.geraldmkilby.com.

CONTENTS

Maps for Print   v

1. Five Klicks Due South   1
2. Colonist Number 897   9
3. Old Town   17
4. Like An Everyday Gal   27
5. Terraforming   39
6. At The Red Rock   49
7. G2 Unit   57
8. NIli Fossae   65
9. Distraction   81
10. Central Logistics   101
11. Dumb Droid   113
12. Smoking Gun   121
13. MASS   127
14. Harsh Environment   135
15. Way Station 29   141
16. Council Session   151
17. Reboot   161
18. Droid Down   175
19. Decennial Celebrations   193
20. You Want Me To Do What?   203
21. Space Station   219
22. Star   231

Afterword   241
Also by Gerald M. Kilby   243
About the Author   245

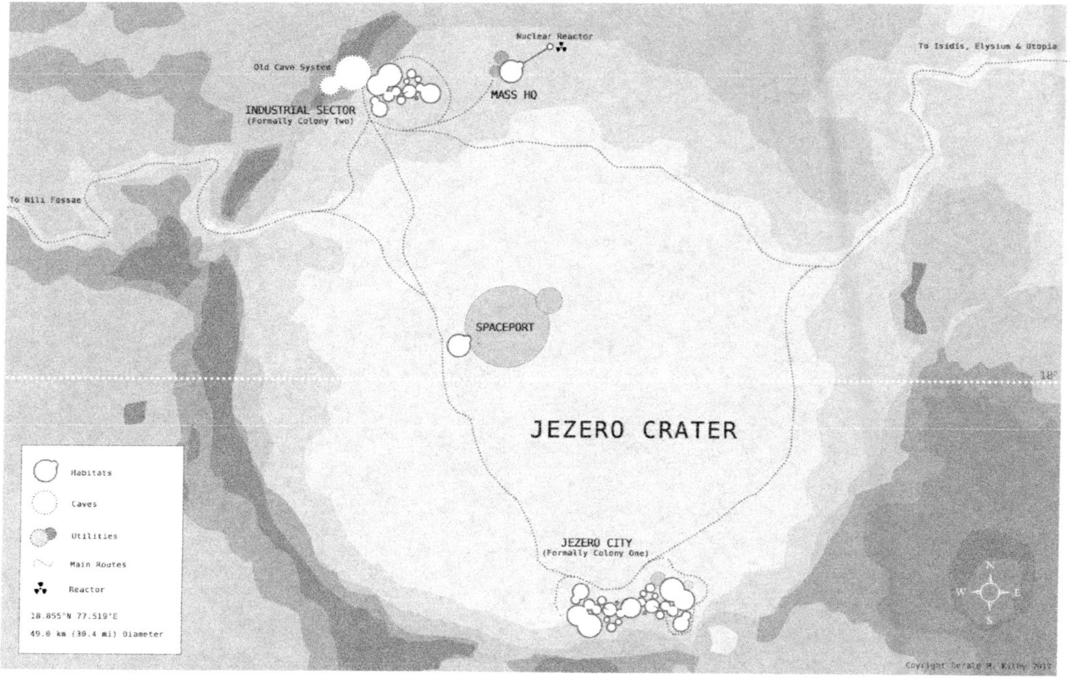
Nuclear Reactor
To Isidis, Elysium & Utopia
Old Cave System
MASS HQ
INDUSTRIAL SECTOR
(Formally Colony Two)
To Nili Fossae
SPACEPORT
18°
JEZERO CRATER
Habitats
Caves
Utilities
Main Routes
Reactor
18.855°N 77.519°E
49.0 km (30.4 mi) Diameter
JEZERO CITY
(Formally Colony One)
N
W
E
S

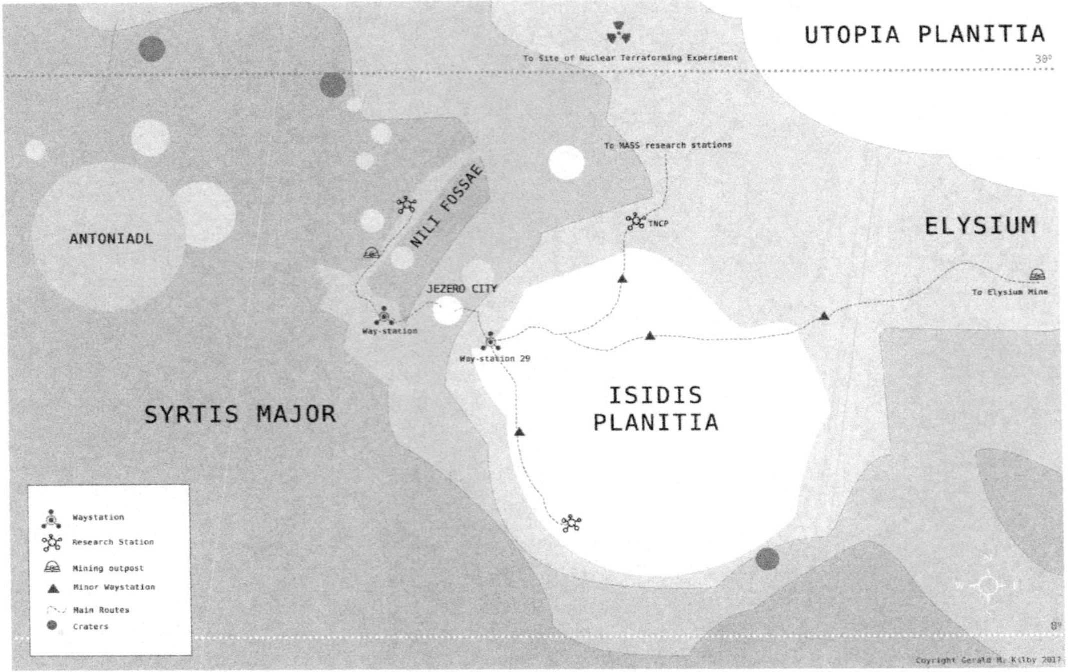
UTOPIA PLANITIA
To Site of Nuclear Terraforming Experiment
30°
To MASS research stations
TNCP
ELYSIUM
To Elysium Mine
ANTONIADL
NILI FOSSAE
JEZERO CITY
Way-station
Way-station 29
ISIDIS PLANITIA
SYRTIS MAJOR
Waystation
Research Station
Mining outpost
Minor Waystation
Main Routes
Craters
8°
Copyright Gerald M. Kilby 2017

1

FIVE KLICKS DUE SOUTH

Jay Eriksen was just five klicks due south of the way station when he first felt a slight change in the rover's operation. Nothing major, just a different sound. But it came with a vaguely troubling vibration, the sort that could be nothing—then again it could mean trouble.

His senses were now on high alert to any further fluctuations in the mechanics of the machine. He was acutely aware that the only thing keeping him alive on Mars was technology, and if some vital component failed, then he would probably die. But he was not unduly worried, since he was nearing his destination: the way station near the entrance to the six-hundred kilometer long Nili Fossae trench.

There were a great many of these way stations, or *relay points*, as they were sometimes called. They radiated out from the main population centers in Jezero Crater and punctuated the routes to the new outposts. A welcome refuge for the weary traveler along the ever expanding Martian highways. The road he was currently on was a well-traveled route, with machines crossing the high central plateau loaded with ore for processing back in Jezero—the epicenter of human colonization on Mars.

Jay knew it well. He had delivered supplies many times to the mining outpost as well as to the various way stations along its route. These were an important component in the fledgling highway infrastructure of Mars. They facilitated longer journeys, expanding the reach of the exploration teams and miners. As on Earth, useful resources were seldom conveniently located on one's doorstep, so long journeys needed to be made to access these resources. Up here, all across Nili Fossae, was an area rich in calcium carbonate, a significant compound in the manufacture of cement. This made the expansion of Jezero possible. Here the raw materials for construction were extracted and transported back down to the Industrial Sector, where it was processed into a thick viscous sludge to be used by the multitude of industrial 3D printing robots that now dominated Jezero's landscape. They worked non-stop, 24/7, or as in the case of Mars 24.5/7, laying down new layers and constructing ever more intricate buildings. The old Colony One, now known as Jezero City, had expanded beyond all recognition over the last decade, and currently housed over nine hundred people.

The construction robots had also been busy

elsewhere. The new Industrial Sector, site of the old Colony Two, had also grown significantly under their ceaseless mechanical hand. It now expanded out from the cave at the base of the crater rim to accommodate the workshops and processing plants of the burgeoning asteroid mining industry that was the main source of Jezero's wealth. Even the vast, formerly empty, space of the central crater basin had not escaped the hand of humanity. Here a two kilometer diameter pad of concrete had been laid down to facilitate a spaceport, with a myriad of ancillary buildings for administration, immigration and technical support hugging its western edge.

Over time, natural roads had been etched out across the crater connecting all these different sectors. They had been created more by constant use than by design. But other natural roads existed, ones created long ago by the geological nature of the planet, back when Jezero was a vast lake. To the west and north, two great channels had been carved into the rock by rivers feeding the lake from the surrounding highlands. To the northeast another natural channel would have drained this primordial lake into the Isidis Planitia, a vast circular lowland plain over fifteen hundred kilometers across. Further out, the northern rim of Isidis merged into the immense, and poetically named, Plains of Utopia. North of this were the research stations of the UN Mars Alliance Scientific Survey (MASS). To the west were the platinum mines in the lee of Elysium Mons, a long extinct volcano some fourteen kilometers high. It was out there that the furthest reaches of humanity's footprint on Mars extended.

Jay Eriksen was one of many couriers, as they were called, moving goods and supplies around the expanding human infrastructure on Mars. He was in essence a truck driver, and the irony was not lost on him, that since more truck driving jobs were being lost to autonomous vehicles on Earth, there were far better prospects for the profession up here on Mars. Yet he would shortly be giving up this life, and finally realizing his dream of returning to Earth. He counted down the sols to his departure.

He had been so immersed in his reverie that he hadn't noticed the temperature alert flashing on his console. It was Banjo, his G2 unit, that brought it to his attention. Banjo was a semi-autonomous droid, designed by the fabled engineer Nills Langthorp, from an original prototype that still existed. That original unit was highly intelligent and virtually sentient. But whatever level of brilliance the original of the G2 species possessed it certainly didn't pass it on. Banjo, like all other mass produced G2 units was as dumb as a bucket of plankton. Its purpose was to lift, move, stack and sort, which it was pretty good at, and it would do it all day long without complaint. It responded to simple voice commands and basic interrogation, but beyond that, one could hardly call it sentient. Jay considered this was probably a good thing. Firstly, the processing power required to maintain a high level of intelligence in all current droids would probably be enormous. But mainly, it would just be a pain in the ass to communicate with. What's more, what would happen if they all got pissed off lifting and stacking and banded together to sue for more rights? The colony would grind to a halt.

"Temperature anomaly in left-hand rear drive transmission," the unit announced.

Jay snapped back to the here and now and looked at the readouts. "Damn." He slowed the rover down.

"How far to the way station, Banjo?"

The G2 unit took a second to respond. "One point six kilometers".

Jay considered his options. If the drive was heating up it could mean a bust bearing. And considering the outside temperature was ridiculously cold, for the drive to be that hot meant it must be pretty bad. If he kept driving it could shatter and he would be stuck here. However, if a fragment from the damaged bearing punctured the skin of the rover, then he would then be losing atmosphere.

He could take a risk and push ahead for the way station, or he could play it safe, stop the rover and do the one point six kilometers on foot. But before he could come to a conclusion, the decision was made for him. A horrendous noise emanated from the rear of the rover as the bearing housing disintegrated.

Smoke filled the cockpit and warnings blared out

from the console as a fire started sucking in oxygen at an alarming rate.

"What the..." he looked over at Banjo. "Put out that fire, Banjo."

The G2 unit spun around to size up the situation. But Jay was beginning to get the feeling that this might be more serious than a bust bearing. He considered that getting the hell out of the rover might be a good thing, at least until the fire was out. That wouldn't take too long as there was only so much oxygen available to feed the flames.

He grabbed his helmet and clipped it on. The visor closed and his EVA suit booted up, checking various stats in sequence. Once he got the green light he hit the button on the rover dash to open the emergency exit on the driver's side. The hatch blew, sucking out all the air and extinguishing the fire. Jay clambered out the opening and down the side of the rover. He had just put both feet on the ground when the machine blew up—completely.

The force sent him sailing through the thin Martian air for quite a distance. He hit the ground, spinning and tumbling around twenty meters from the blast. He was lying on his back looking directly up at the sky. Across his field of vision he could see a hairline crack begin to snake its way across his visor. He instinctively raised a hand to cover it, he could hear a faint hiss of escaping air. He raised himself up and looked back at the blackened husk of the rover. He could just make out the dismembered remains of Banjo scattered about. *This is not good*, he thought. But he still had a chance, he could try to get to the way station before his oxygen ran out.

He forced himself to move. *Up, get up, get moving.* He stood up, and staggered. He was very unsteady, his legs were like jelly. *You're just in shock, it will pass, now go.* He moved with a faltering gait at first but as his mind began to focus more he found a rhythm, one foot in front of the other.

He picked his way up out of the gully he had been thrown into by the blast. It was difficult as every now and again he would remove his hand from the visor to get his balance and would hear the faint hiss again. By the time he scrambled back up onto the road his EVA suit was flashing a low oxygen warning. Something was wrong. Even with the cracked visor it shouldn't be losing air at this rate. It was at that moment that Jay began to panic, as the full implications of his predicament began to sink in.

He wasn't going to make it to the way station. Maybe he'd get halfway there, but that wasn't good enough—he might as well be a million miles away. There were no half measures on Mars. He couldn't radio for help as his EVA suit didn't have the range. He sank down to his knees. There was no two ways about this. He was going to die, and there wasn't a damn thing he could do about it.

2

COLONIST NUMBER 897

Mia Sorelli, colonist number 897, hefted a full box of tomatoes onto a robotic transport pallet and tapped the screen on her slate to instruct it to move the load to storage. It reversed out from its position at her side and glided off to a predetermined location in the food processing sector. This was her first load of the sol. She scanned her slate again to check where she should go to next. A long list of tasks scrolled up her screen, color coded for resource requirements, and indexed for credit value and knowledge points earned. The list had already been filtered for her particular skill level by central processing, and since she had only been here a few months, her level was pretty low—she still had a lot to learn.

It had initially taken Mia quite a while to get her head around the basics of how people worked in the colony. Rather than being assigned a specific job, each colonist could choose from a wide range of tasks which were within their skill level. So she could stay here and pack more tomatoes or she could opt for a change of scenery, and head off to one of the other sectors that needed an extra pair of hands. As each task was completed it was tagged, cataloged and fed back into *central*. The colonist would then gain some skill points and central would recalibrate the list of task options presented.

To a newly arrived colonist such as Mia this seemed a chaotic system, considering a great many of these tasks could be better served by a robot, and they had no shortage of industrial servants. But after a few weeks of this work she began to see the method in the madness. The two most important things up here, apart from having air to breathe, were food and social cohesion. Of those, food production was number one on the list. Without food there would be no colony, it was sacrosanct. It was the only thing that really mattered, with the entire colony one-hundred percent focused on this singular task —growing as much food as possible, never stopping and constantly expanding production. Already seventy percent of the physical infrastructure here was designated for growing, processing or storing food.

After a while Mia began to understand that if all this planting, tending, picking, and packing were to be performed solely by automation then the social fabric of the colony would start to collapse. So, by having everybody involved, nobody felt like they were not needed. If you didn't like a particular task or didn't like the people you were working with, you could hop off somewhere else. You didn't need to ask, it was your choice, you were empowered. It was also a great way to meet new people, listen to their stories, and make new friends.

Not only did this work physically sustain the population, it was the glue that bound them together socially. Everybody had to take part, no exceptions, even the original colonists, the pioneers as some called them. It kept everybody grounded. It was like one big high-tech socialist commune, at least on the surface. But dive underneath and it became clear to Mia that some very clever algorithms based on market economics were working feverishly in the background to prioritize tasks and motivate colonists.

Tasks would go up or down the list in terms of urgency. As they did, they became more valuable to the colonist, with greater credits and skill points being attached to them. This meant that simpler or more pleasant tasks were not worth as much as the more complex or unpleasant tasks. But even if all colonists chose to opt for the more arduous tasks their value would drop as the labour supply rose. In tandem with this, other tasks would rise in value as labour became scarce. It was a form of gamification, and after a while Mia began to see how everybody trusted the system to alert them to what needed to be done and when, so that the colony could grow and prosper—and ultimately nobody would starve to death. Once Mia got a handle on the weird working system, she took to it like a bird on the wing and began to soar. Already she had leveled up several times, which also meant a whole new range of training options were now opening up to her.

It had been a bold decision to come here, one where she had many sleepless nights wondering if she were really making the right choice in opting to become a colonist. But now all that doubt had faded away and Mia had begun to feel good about life again; she even had a relationship on the brew. But most of all, she had finally put the horror of her past behind her. It was something that, in the darkest moments of her previous life, she never thought possible.

She checked her slate again. *Hmmm... strawberries. Always nice for a change.* She tapped on the task list, put her slate back in her pocket, and headed off to a different sector. She still had some time to kill, so rather than going directly to her next task, she made a detour along the main avenue of Jezero City. This was a rather grandiose name for what was essentially a domed area that connected several sectors together. It was a junction, with a wide main walkway that bisected the space. On either side were small, semi-circular gardens with seating and fountains. Around the inner perimeter was another walkway with a cafe, a bar of sorts, and a kind of proto-market, where the fledgling consumer economy of the colony had started to take root. There were small stalls with food and handcrafted artifacts. Central were actively encouraging this retail commerce, and it seemed to be working as there was always something new popping up on the Avenue. Ironically, it was the artifacts from Earth that had the highest value. Odd items, like the humble pen or a pad of paper were wildly expensive—if counted in colony credits.

The Avenue was busy at this time. The first tasks of the morning were over and colonists were now in transit between sectors. It looked to Mia like they all decided to do exactly as she had planned and head for the Avenue. At the far end a large stage and a big screen were being erected for the upcoming decennial celebrations. It would be ten years since the colony on Mars gained its independence from Earth and there was going to be a party. Mia could already feel the excitement building in the population as the time drew closer.

"The Avenue seems very alive this sol."

Mia turned to identify the source of the comment. Standing beside her was a tall thin man in his thirties. He smiled at her and nodded towards the giant screen that was being hauled up into position. "Won't be long now before the celebrations start."

Mia smiled back at him. "Yeah."

She pegged him as one of the original colonists, a Pioneer. He had that thin stretched look that seemed to be a common trait amongst them. Mia wondered if living for so long in one third gravity made them like that. Or was it the weird genetics that they possessed? She often thought about this. The history she had heard seemed to be a confusing mix of myth and fact. Some said they were immortal, a quirk of the genetic experiments that these early colonists had been subjected to. Mia thought that this was probably bullshit. Nonetheless, there was no denying the horrors they must all have endured to make the colony what it was now. A place where hardship was defined by lack of access to some decent lipstick.

"Are you Mia Sorelli?"

Mia looked around and considered this question for moment. "Yes. And you?"

"You can call me Werren." He extended a thin skeletal hand. Mia shook it, surprised that its fragile appearance belied its strong grip.

"I'm here to inform you that someone... important would like to have a talk with you. I'm to escort you there now."

Mia stepped back, gave the enigmatic colonist a long considered look and raised a hand. "Sorry pal, this is all a bit too cloak and dagger for me. You'll need to give me a better story than that. Anyway, I hate to break it to you but I've got to go back to work shortly."

He was unfazed by her reaction. "My apologies if it all seems a bit clandestine, but this is important. If you check your slate you'll find you're clear for the rest of the sol."

Mia fished her slate out of her pocket and checked her list. Sure enough, she was free until tomorrow. Whoever this *someone* was, they had to have some clout. She stuffed it back in her pocket. "So tell me who it is then."

"I'd rather not say," he glanced around, "...not here. But suffice to say she is very anxious to meet you."

"She?" Mia cocked an eyebrow.

"Yes."

"Well that narrows it down a bit."

"To fifty percent of the population, I would guess."

"Less than that, Werren. If they can clear my slate for the sol, then I would say it narrows it down to around a half-dozen people."

He gave a subtle smile along with a slight tilt of his head. "Very astute."

"Not really. I just get the impression you're trying to tell me enough to get me interested, that's all.

He smiled again. "Like I said, very astute."

Mia stood for a moment and considered this encounter. What signals was she getting? The pioneer had his hood up and kept glancing around at the crowd of colonists passing up and down the Avenue. Was he afraid of being recognized by someone? Mia couldn't put her finger on it. He wasn't hiding, but then again, he wasn't advertising himself either. With his hood up he could pass for any number of other colonists. And he had even given her a few good clues as to who wanted to meet her, but stopped short of coming straight out with it. However, she didn't get any sense of danger. But her internal warning antennae were still not fully up to speed in this new environment, so she could be missing something. What the hell was going on? In the end, there was only one way to find out.

"Okay, what the heck. Come on, let's go find out who wants to talk to me so badly."

Werren nodded. "Okay, do you know where the grain silos are located?"

"Yeah, over in Ag Sector Three."

"If you follow the corridor past the silos to the very end, I'll meet you there in say... twenty minutes?"

Mia shrugged. "Sure."

He smiled again, then turned and walked off into the crowd.

Mia just stood watching him as he disappeared. *Well that was weird.*

3

OLD TOWN

Mia had done very little exploration of Jezero City since she arrived on the planet. She also thought that it was a bit of a stretch to call it a city, since only around nine hundred people lived here, around two-thirds of the total population of Mars. In some respects it was like a small village on Earth, with the rump of the population clustered around a small commercial center, and agricultural radiating outward. But unlike Earth, Jezero City had to enclose all this in one gigantic maze of domed structures, this being the simplest and most efficient shape for the 3D printers to manufacture. But even with this basic shape there was still a bewildering variety of styles, from the small units built for utilities to the giant structures for food production.

The great biodome, once the primary architectural feature of the old Colony One, was now lost in the skyline of the new city. Swallowed up by the widening perimeter of new domes. Like honeycomb in the hive, once the mechanical insects of Jezero had finished creating one sector, it was straight on to the next. Looking down from orbit it must seem like a great mound of blisters blooming out across the skin of the crater.

Of course, none of this higgledy-piggledy ad-hoc construction made any sense to Mia. It seemed to her that new sectors were simply added as they were needed, rather than with any regard to a master plan. In many ways this made it more interesting as you never knew what lay just around the proverbial corner, and since new ships arrived every six months, disgorging another hundred souls into the city, there was always a sense of excitement in the air.

THE CORRIDOR she now found herself in connected several agri-domes together. It was wide and busy, mainly with robotic traffic moving produce and materials between other sectors. At the far end were two large grain silos, one on either side. She continued down the length of the corridor until it came to a dead end, terminating at an airlock. She peered in through the small window in the door. It was a rover dock. A utility where transports could connect directly to the city infrastructure, thereby negating the need to EVA. Both airlock doors could then be opened and goods brought in and out in a full pressure environment. This was critical for perishable

Jezero City

goods, as any exposure to the harsh Martian environment could ruin all but the very hardiest of raw produce.

Mia could see a rover had been docked, and she could also see all the way down its interior into the cockpit. Werren was sitting in the pilot seat, talking into his headset. He finally noticed her looking in and raised a finger to let her know he'd be with her in a moment. Mia stood back from the door and waited. *What the hell am I getting myself into here?* she thought. *Looks like I'm going on a trip.* But before she had time to get cold feet and walk away, the door swung open.

"Miss Sorelli, you came. True to your word." Werren stepped back and waved an arm to usher her into the machine. It was the first time Mia had been in a rover since landing on the planet. Then, they had simply been ferried from the ship over to the immigration and processing facilities out at the edge of the spaceport apron. Her memories of that journey consisted of trying to cope with the sudden effect of gravity on her body. She then spent a few sols acclimatizing in processing, before being piled onto a rover and ferried to Jezero City to start her new life. It was a journey she remembered vividly. Mia and several other colonists had their faces stuck to the windows of the rover, like a school of sucker fish in a tank, watching as the great domes of Jezero City rose up from the horizon.

She strapped herself into one of the passenger seats beside Werren as he disengaged the rover from the airlock and moved out from Ag-sector. Ahead of her, Mia could see the wide expanse of the crater stretching off into the distance. To her left she could see along the northern edge of the city. Here and there giant 3D printers were busy laying down new structures. Further out she spotted several other rovers of varying types, moving along the northern road across the crater. This led to the site of the original Colony Two, now called the Industrial Sector, and further up to the mines at Nili Fossae.

She turned back to Werren. "So, where are we going?"

The rover veered east, and Werren nodded at a direction vaguely forward. "Over there, Old Town."

"Old Town?"

"Eh... you call it Central." he replied.

"Never heard it called Old Town, kinda cute."

Mia immediately regretted saying that, as she could tell he wasn't impressed with it being described as *kinda cute*.

"In a deep and meaningful way, of course," she tried to claw her way back.

He stayed silent, a sullen look painted on his face.

"I hate to be the one to break this to you, Werren, but we could have walked there. Not that I don't appreciate you taking me out for a drive and all that."

He gave her a look as if to say, *do me a favor and shut up*.

"But of course, lots of people would have seen us strolling along together, not to mention all those cameras everywhere," she added.

Werren remained silent.

"But this way, it's all on the QT. Someone is going to a lot of trouble to hide any evidence of this meeting."

"It's just quicker this way, that's all," he answered finally.

"Really?"

"Yes, really."

Mia gave him a look but decided to cut him a break and sit back and enjoy the ride. It wasn't often it happened and only a lucky few who get in to Old Town. This was what the original colony grew out of, where the very first biodome was constructed. It was still there, but greatly expanded. If the rumors were to be believed it was now a kind of retirement home for the pioneers. Although, Mia reckoned that too was probably bullshit. Nevertheless, the sector she was about to enter was the governmental and administrative heart of the entire human colony on Mars. Here was where the council met, and where many of the councilors lived, along with an army of administrators, technicians and bureaucrats that managed the sol-to-sol running of the colony. They were generally known to everybody simply as Central.

Old Town, Mia thought. It sounded like this went deeper than just Central. Old Town smacked of secrets and subterfuge, where the myth and the politics of the history of the colony's founding were kept in glass cases, preserved and polished, lest they be forgotten by those who think it's all *kinda cute*.

She could see the fabled biodome coming into view

as the rover skirted the last edges of the new city. The dome was smaller than she had imagined. Perhaps its legend had made it bigger in the mind than it actually was in reality. All around its perimeter were the main administrative buildings for Central. Behind the biodome, stretching back towards the crater rim, a large three story building rose up. Along its facade Mia could see a wide ribbon of windows facing out on the city. *Must be one hell of a view from up there*, she thought.

Werren brought the rover up to the base of this building and reversed into a vacant dock. It came to a halt with a satisfying clunk and a hiss as the airlock engaged.

"We're here. Come, follow me."

They exited the rover into a plush circular atrium. The floor was covered in a thick hessian carpet, the first time Mia had seen such luxurious flooring anywhere in Jezero. There were plants and small trees scattered around the space. In the center, a small fountain trickled water over a pebbled pond. Light flooded in from a glass canopy above.

"Nice digs. How can I get me one of these?"

"Maybe when you grow up."

Mia looked over at Werren and gave him a wide grin. "See, I knew you had a sense of humor buried in there somewhere."

He smiled back as he held his palm against a panel on the far wall. Doors slid open to reveal a lift. They stepped inside, the door closed and the lift rose—all the way to the top, as far as Mia could figure. The doors finally opened directly into a wide open living space.

Werren gestured for her to exit the lift. "This is where I must leave you."

Mia hesitated for a moment, then stepped out. The far wall was a single, wide window looking out over the domed city and across the central crater plateau. The silhouette of a woman with her back to Mia, stood looking out at the grand vista. She had one hand up to her ear, talking to someone. For a few moments Mia wasn't sure what to do, and gave a startled jump when the lift doors closed behind her. This seemed to alert the woman to her presence and she turned around to greet her.

"Ah... Mia Sorelli, so glad you could come."

Mia recognized her immediately. She guessed that she would be meeting someone important, someone from the council or high up in Central. But what she didn't expect was to be meeting the legend that was Dr. Jann Malbec.

Mia's mouth opened, but nothing came out. And for the first time in a great many months, Mia was speechless.

"Please, come in, take a seat. Can I get you anything, something to drink perhaps?"

Mia tried to force some words out of her mouth, anything would do. Her brain was sending the signals, but nothing was happening.

"Please forgive all the mystery. I'm sure it seems a bit over the top."

"Eh... yes... a drink would be great."

Jann moved over to within arm's reach of Mia and offered her hand. "I'm Dr. Jann Malbec, thank you for coming."

Mia looked down and then shook her hand. Jann held it for a moment as she directed the hapless Mia to a low chair by the window. "Please, have a seat." She released her grip. Mia sat and tried to regain some composure, and she was getting there until an odd looking G2 unit whizzed into the room and stopped beside Dr. Malbec.

"Ah... Gizmo, good of you to join us. This is Mia Sorelli, the one I was telling you about."

The droid swiveled its head and looked at Mia as if it was doing a full body scan on her. It then raised one arm and spoke. "Greetings, Earthling."

"Eh... greetings." Mia managed to reply.

"Gizmo, would you be so kind as to fetch us some tea?" Jann asked the droid as she moved herself to a seat opposite Mia.

"Certainly." It whizzed out of the main room leaving a stunned Mia watching it go.

"That's quite a quirky G2 unit you've got there."

Dr. Malbec picked up a slate, scanned the screen then looked up at Mia. "Yes, but it's not a G2 unit. It's actually the original that all the others are based on. That's what the G in G2 stands for. *Gizmo.*"

"If it's a '2,' then there must have been a one before it?"

Dr. Malbec nodded. "Yes, there was." She waved a dismissive hand. "But that was a long time ago now." She watched the droid come back in with a tray and place it deftly on a low table between them.

"Thank you, Gizmo." Jann handed a cup to Mia.

"No problem, catch you all later." And it whizzed off again.

Mia was still watching. "It's not like the others, is it?"

Dr. Malbec gave a slight laugh. "No, that's for sure." She sat back in her seat. "Anyway, as I said, thanks for agreeing to meet me. I'm sure you're wondering what it's all about."

"The thought had crossed my mind."

Malbec consulted her slate again and swiped a finger across its surface. "So, you've been here, what... nearly seven months now?"

"Yeah."

Malbec looked up. "And how's it going, I mean, how are you getting on?"

Mia gave a brief nod. "Keeping the head down, going to bed early, being a good girl... for the most part."

Malbec shifted in her chair. Mia reckoned this wasn't the answer she was expecting. "It can be a difficult transition for many. Some people take time to adjust to this new life," Jann said.

"I imagine so."

"But you haven't had any problem, with the transition, that is?"

Mia looked at Dr. Malbec for a moment, then carefully set her cup back down on the table. She sat back in the chair and put her hands on the armrests. "Correct me if I'm wrong, Dr. Malbec..."

"Jann. Please call me Jann."

"Jann. I'm guessing you didn't go to all the trouble to get me here just to do a one woman survey of the local citizenry?"

Jann paused a beat before replying, "No, you're right... I didn't."

"Well then, why don't you just spit it out and tell me whatever it is you brought me here for."

Jann sat back in her chair and looked out the window for a moment. "I need your help."

4

LIKE AN EVERYDAY GAL

Dr. Jann Malbec looked out the window at the domed skyline of Jezero City. "You know the type of people that we have up here, Mia?"

Mia didn't answer, preferring instead to let Dr. Malbec do the talking.

"Engineers and scientists—all highly skilled. It's this way because of our selection process, only the best of the best get to become colonists." She looked around at Mia. "But you came here on the lottery system. So that makes you one of the eight percent of colonists that are essentially picked at random."

"So I'm not a scientist, not the *best of the best*. Is that what you wanted to tell me?" Mia finally found her voice again.

Dr. Malbec sat back down and picked up her slate. "No, you're not a scientist, this is true. But you do have a unique skill set that no one else up here has. And you're one of the best in your field."

"And what field would that be?"

Dr. Malbec swiped her finger across the slate again and tapped on something. "You worked as a homicide investigator for six years before that... unfortunate incident ended your career."

Unfortunate incident. Mia's gut churned at the memory. It was something she had tried very hard to bury deep within herself for the last five years. She had left it behind when she strapped herself into the colony ship and departed Earth. Now this bitch was dragging it back up again. Who the hell did she think she was?

"Look, lady. I know you're something of a big cheese here, but you can't go trawling through the dirty laundry of a colonist. It's supposed to be like the French Foreign Legion on Mars, you leave all the dirt behind on Earth, and no one gets to use it. Christ, I thought there was a law against that sort of thing here?" Mia was shocked at her own outburst. She didn't handle it very well and now she had ruined any advantage she might have gained from her meeting with one of the most powerful people on the planet.

Dr. Malbec quietly placed the slate back down on the table and regarded Mia. "You're right. While poking into people's *dirty laundry* is not exactly against the law here, it is very much discouraged, unless there is a clear need to do so. And I have a need that you happen to be uniquely equipped to undertake."

Mia had regained some of her composure. She took a few more sips of tea just to distract herself a bit and help her get a grip. "I'm sorry, Dr. Malbec. But it's a bit of a touchy subject for me."

"Why don't you tell me about it?"

Mia pointed at the slate resting on the table between them. "Do I really need to? You already know all about it. You probably know more about me than I do myself."

"Look, Mia. We all have our shit. Stuff we want to forget, things we wish never happened. But it's not about the crap, it's about how we deal with it that matters."

"Easy for you to say, you're a goddamn legend."

"Trust me, that has its disadvantages."

They both got quiet for a moment before Jann spoke again. "Why don't you just tell me about it yourself, about what happened to you."

Mia sighed. It was not something she really wanted to get into, not now, not ever. But there was something about Dr. Malbec. Perhaps it was because she had been through more crap than anyone could ever hope to survive. And yet, here she was, in the flesh, drinking tea, just like an everyday gal. Mia never had anything but respect for her and what she had accomplished. But maybe it was because her own personal traumas paled in comparison to Dr. Malbec's dark past, that she finally let it all out. The first time she had done so in over five years.

"I killed an innocent kid. Shot her with my service pistol. It was my finger that pulled the trigger." There, she said it.

She looked up at Malbec and shrugged. "It was an accident, just one of those things. She was in the wrong place at the wrong time." Mia sighed, sat back in the chair and proceeded to tell her story.

"I was following up on a lead, checking out a lowlife who was a known associate of a guy we were looking for. He was holed up in a dump on the outskirts. It was a big old block, falling apart, full of poor families living on the edge. Anyway, I headed over there on my own. That was my first mistake. Someone somewhere tipped him off I was coming. You know the way these places work. They see a cop coming in through the lobby and all of a sudden the pipes start rattling. By the time I'd reached the third floor, he was ready and waiting. He jumped me in the stairwell, and punched me in the face. I went flying, and he took off like a fat torpedo. Once I got my head together I took off after him."

"He was a big bastard, so he was slow. I had him in my sights by the time I got to the ground floor, so I pulled out my weapon and shouted a warning at him. There were a bunch of other people around who all hit the floor at this point. He didn't stop, so I ran after him and then... well, I tripped over some guy on the ground taking cover. I never found out if he did it deliberately, you know—so the other guy could get away. Anyway, I fell to the floor, and the gun went off.

"For a moment or two there was complete silence. Then the screaming started. I pulled myself up and went over to see what had happened. A young mother was cradling a kid in her arms, blood seeping from a wound in the girl's abdomen. She was still alive then. I remember her eyes staring up at me, as if to say *why did you kill me...* and her mother screaming, screaming, screaming." Mia put her head in her hands and let a few moments go by before she wiped her face and continued.

"Then they shot me. Never found out who it was. I took a bullet in the chest and one in my left shoulder. I don't remember anything after that until I woke up to a shitstorm. The kid was an immigrant, so I was a racist bitch and all the goddamn politics of the moment got dumped down on my head. They destroyed me. Screwed me over and hung me out to swing."

Mia shook her head. "Then for two years I looked for escape in the bottom of a bottle and a drawer full of pills —I didn't find any. Sometimes I thought it would have been better if they had convicted me for something and locked me up. Anyway, bit by bit I pulled myself back together. Once I had climbed out from the bottom of the pit some friends lent a hand and straightened me out. That's when I started getting interested in the colony."

She looked at Jann. "It's hard to ignore the colony back on Earth, it's everywhere. So, I said what the heck, couldn't be worse than this place. I applied, and the department, to their credit, decided to sponsor me. I think they felt bad about all the crap that had been dished out to me. Anyway, I got picked in the lottery and... well, here I am—that's my story."

Jann sat back and sighed deeply. "That's a lot of bad luck."

"I know, I know. It's easy to say, but once the media get you in their sights you're no longer a human being, you're just a story, and they'll milk it for all they can get—then spit you out, a spent husk, nothing left of you to matter to anyone."

"I know that feeling."

"Yeah, that's probably the only reason I'm telling you all this. I know you get what it really feels like."

They sat for a while, saying nothing. Finally Mia reached for the tea, held it up towards Jann. "I don't suppose you have something a bit stronger than tea?"

Jann smiled. "Sure. I think I have something you might like." She rose from her seat and wandered out of the room for a few minutes. Mia felt like she had just run a marathon. She was exhausted, but surprisingly elated, like a great weight had been taken off her shoulders. She had somehow opened a new door, moved on, leveled up.

Jann came back holding two glasses, and offered one to Mia, who accepted it and took a sip. Her eyes widened. "Oh my god, is this what I think it is?"

"Kentucky bourbon, all the way from Earth. It's the real deal." Jann sat down again, picked up the slate and waved it at Mia. "It says here it's your favorite."

Mia raised her glass to Jann. "Here's to Mars."

"To Mars."

After a brief period of delicate sipping and savoring her drink Mia set it down on the table, brushed the creases out of her colony issue jumpsuit and clasped her hands in her lap. "So, what is it you want me to do?"

Jann held her gaze for a moment, like she was considering how best to spit it out. Mia dearly hoped that she wouldn't have to sit through a potted history of the Mars colony.

"I want you to investigate a murder."

"A murder? Well that's a big ask." Mia shook her head a few times. "I'm not sure I can be any help to you—even if I agreed to do it."

Jann raised a hand. "Just hear me out, Mia. Then you can decide."

Mia extended her hands as if to say *go right ahead*, and sat back. "Okay, but I can tell you right now, I'm not doing it."

"You probably heard about the courier that was killed on a resupply mission over at Nili Fossae?"

"Yeah, tragic. I heard his rover blew up," said Mia

"Well, I'm not so sure it was an accident."

"Got any evidence to support that hypothesis?" Mia took another sip of her drink.

"No. That's why I need someone to investigate it."

Mia pursed her lips. "I feel like I'm being dragged into something that frankly I want no part of. But, since we're buddies now, and I haven't finished this very delicious bourbon, I'll humor you with a few of the more obvious questions. The first being, why do you think it's not simply an accident?"

"Rovers don't blow up like that. Yes, there have been

fatalities in the past, due to system failures, or even just plain stupidity. But this was catastrophic."

"That's not evidence, Jann. At best it's just *unusual*." Mia picked up her drink and took another sip. It might be a long long time before she ever had a drink like this, so she was going to savor it for as long as possible. "Next question, and this is the most fundamental, why would someone want this courier dead?"

Jann sighed. "I don't know. That's the problem. I don't really know what's going on. I've either lost touch with the sociopolitical zeitgeist of the colony or someone is hiding something from me."

"Well, we have a word for that where I come from. It's called paranoia. Maybe you just need to get out more."

Jann let out a laugh and began to nod her head. Eventually she stood up and walked over to the window again. "Maybe you're right, Mia. Perhaps I've spent too long cooped up in this ivory tower, looking down on my realm, trying to divine some nefarious meaning in every random event." She stood there for a while, just looking out. Finally she turned back to Mia. "Great change is happening."

Oh God, here it comes, thought Mia. *The history lesson.* She sipped her drink just to remind herself why she was prepared to listen to Dr. Malbec drone on.

"It's been nearly thirty years since the first colonist set foot on the planet. We've come a long way since then. And in less than a week we will celebrate the tenth anniversary of our independence from Earth, the decennial. Still, Earth continues to try and undermine our independence. This last decade of autonomy has been fought over every single day by the UN. "

Mia was tempted to say, *well that's a bummer*, but she refrained. Instead she simply said, "I see."

"The decennial also marks the end of the exclusive mining and transit concessions given to AsterX."

"AsterX, who are they?" Mia felt she was being drawn in against her will.

Jann turned away from her window gazing and sat back down. Mia realized she might be here for a while longer. Perhaps she could prompt Jann for another shot, just to ease the passage.

"AsterX is an asteroid mining company. Our independence came at a price, and that was granting exclusive mining and transit rights to AsterX. They've prospered greatly from it, but we too have benefited greatly from this arrangement. All that is now coming to an end. Mars is opening up. For the past year, dozens of space corporations have been lobbying for these new concessions. We're entering the next phase of our development and the growth will be... exponential."

"Well, that's great, surely?"

Jann shook her head. "Yes and no. You see..."

Mia instantly regretted letting her mouth take over her brain. Now she had given Dr. Malbec an opportunity to really get going. She took another sip and resigned herself to being here for a while longer.

"...my big fear is keeping control of this explosion of

growth. With so many interested parties vying for position it's extremely difficult to see the wood for the trees—politically and socially. There are powerful interests who would like nothing more than to see the colony here return to direct control of Earth."

"Jann..." Mia had had enough. She had no interest in politics and she got the feeling that Dr. Jann Malbec had spent too long fretting over the machinations of those around her to be able to see anything of the reality. "...what's all this got to do with the dead guy?"

Jann sighed. "If someone or some group wanted to take back control of the colony then the time to do that is running out. After the decennial celebrations, and when the AsterX concessions end, it will be too late."

"That's not an answer. That's simply a personal fear, Jann. Okay, let's say that this guy was murdered. Who stands to gain from it?"

"That I don't know. But a rover does not just blow up like that."

"Look, if you want my professional opinion, you're chasing ghosts. You're falling into the trap of trying to bend facts to fit your own hypothesis. You need to ask yourself the hard question, *am I just being paranoid?*"

"You're not convinced?"

Mia laughed. "Very thin pickings, Jann. There's nothing you've said so far that leads me to think this was anything more than an unfortunate accident."

"Well, don't you see? That's why I need someone to investigate it."

Mia shook her head. "No. I'm sorry, but I'm not your girl." She put her now finished glass back down on the table and leaned in a bit. Her voice was low and hesitant. "Jann, I'll be straight with you. I can't go back there. I left all that behind. What little skill I had died back when I killed that kid. I can't do what you want... I'm not going to let all that in again."

Jann sighed, visibly deflated. Mia could see she was disappointed. Instinctively she wanted to give her something to lessen the blow.

"Listen, I'm not saying your hunch is wrong. Maybe this guy was murdered. Let's face it, you know infinitely more than I do about what's going on up here, so maybe there's something in what you say. It's just... I can't help you. I'm sorry."

"It's okay, I understand."

"Anyway, what good would I be? I've only been here seven months. I'm still finding my way around, haven't even been out of Jezero City. You need someone who knows the ropes. What about the guy who brought me here? He seemed pretty good at snooping around."

"Werren's loyal and very capable but he would be too easily recognized by a great many of the colonists here. I need someone who wouldn't attract attention, not seen to be affiliated to any group or faction."

"Politics again?"

"Life is politics, Mia. Anywhere you get more than two people together, there's politics. It's the consequence of being a species that can communicate."

"Well, I've always done my level best to avoid it, and there was a heck of a lot of it back in the department."

"And how did that work out?"

Mia thought about that for a moment before realizing the point Malbec was trying to make. "Not very well."

"You see Mia, that's the thing about politics. Either you're playing the game, or it's playing you." With this, Jann rose from her seat. Mia sensed the meeting was over. "Thanks for coming."

Mia stood up and shook Jann's outstretched hand. "Sorry I couldn't be of any help."

"That's okay. You've actually helped me more than you think. Werren will take you back."

"Thanks."

"Listen, just one more thing before you go."

"Sure, what is it?

"This meeting never happened. I trust you'll keep our conversation to yourself."

Mia nodded. "You can count on it."

With that, the lift door opened and Werren ushered her in. As the doors closed and the lift descended, Mia got the distinct feeling that this was not the last of it, that Dr. Jann Malbec was not someone you simply walked away from. What she had said about the department politics not being good to her hit a raw nerve. Malbec was cunning, she knew exactly how to jangle Mia's tender area. She had been played for a patsy back on Earth, she could see that more clearly with each passing sol. But she was not going to let that happen again, no goddamn way.

5

TERRAFORMING

In the early years of the colony, the great biodome was constructed for the sole purpose of food production. With it came the first expansion of what was up until then nothing more than an outpost. Momentous as this small human presence was, it was tenuous at best. But since the early colonists had come here on a one-way ticket, they possessed a tenacious drive to secure and fortify their fragile colony. The construction of this biodome was a significant moment in the foundation history, a moment when those who clung to life on this far off planet could realistically call it home. So it possessed a deeper significance to the colonists than any other building that now radiated out across Jezero City.

For a long time, the architecture of the biodome dominated the colony infrastructure, but now it was dwarfed by the massive agri-domes that had been constructed since independence. Yet to the colonists in general, and the pioneers in particular, the biodome was their core. The root from which all else grew. So it came as no surprise to everyone that this was eventually chosen as the central council chamber—the seat of power.

The hydroponics and factory grow beds had been removed and replaced with a lush green garden. The wide central dais now housed a circular array of seating and monitors for use when the council was in session. In the dead center of all this was a large holo-table used to display maps and data, and even the odd holo-cast from Earth, and other agencies that possessed such technology.

It was in this section of the biodome that some of the oldest living plants on Mars existed. Some were giant palms, coconut and banana, their large fronds affording shade across the council dais. On certain sols, the biodome was open to the public and the new citizens of Jezero City could wander and delight in this old established tropical garden. Especially the young, those who were born here, of which there were now around twenty-seven ranging in age from a few months, to the oldest boy, the first Martian. He was now seven Earth years old.

And like all great civilizations it had its statues and monuments. Several larger than life figures greeted the people as they entered. Figures who had played a significant role in the history of the colony. Of course there was a statue of the first human colonist to set foot on Mars. One of Xenon Hybrid, the reclusive, and some would say eccentric President of Mars. There were others, but perhaps the most famous of these was a somewhat controversial statue of a feral and semi-naked Dr. Jann Malbec, her hair in matted dreadlocks, holding a spear above her shoulder, ready to strike. It was a depiction of her time living alone on Mars, in this very biodome where she had regressed to barely more than that of a stone-age hunter. Some colonists hated it. Arguing that such an important figure in the history of the colony as Dr. Malbec, should be depicted so crudely was not proper. But Dr. Malbec herself liked it. She said it was real, she had been that person. She also appreciated it because, in her mind, it showed that despite all our technological brilliance as a species, take it away and we're just animals.

Also in the tropical vegetation surrounding the central council dais were a number of small contemplative spaces, where one could sit and not be overheard. They were used as side meeting areas where sticky political issues could be worked out in private.

In one such area Councilor Yuto Yamashita and Lane Zebos, CEO of the asteroid mining company AsterX were admiring the small fountain that had recently been installed. At its rim a small bird hopped uncertainly before dipping its beak to take a drink. It was one of the few avian species that had survived the journey from Earth. Their songs echoed off the dome and augmented the sense of tropical beauty that the biodome evoked. Their introduction had initially been as a potential additional food source, but as time went by the colony had released some into the space, purely for the aesthetic. While they did indeed add a new layer of beauty to the ecosystem it came with a cost, that being the danger of being in the line of fire when nature called. Lane gave the seat a quick inspection to ensure it was free of guano before seating himself on the stone plinth.

"So Yuto, I'm assuming your request for a quiet chat here was not for us to enjoy the twitter of birds."

"I just wanted to give you a heads up on the unfortunate incident over at Nili Fossae." Yuto kept his eyes on the bird still drinking at the fountain.

"Ahh... yes. A tragic accident I believe."

Yuto shifted his gaze to Lane and lowered his voice. "There are those who are not so sure that this was an accident. They feel that someone or some agency must have sabotaged his rover to make it explode like that."

Lane held Yuto's stare for a beat. "Do they have any evidence to support this theory?"

"No. But here's the thing. That rover was last serviced only one week ago at your shipyard over at the Industrial Sector."

"Meaning?"

Yuto shrugged. "Meaning some individual... who shall remain nameless for the moment... thinks that AsterX might have been behind it."

Lane bent in close to Yuto. "That's horseshit. Why would we even contemplate such a thing?"

"Look, Lane, I know it's crap, I'm simply letting you know it's out there in the wild now."

"Who's spreading this around?"

Yuto waved a hand. "I can't say, but I think you can guess."

Lane sighed and shook his head.

Yuto continued, "As you probably know the rover belonged to the Mars Alliance Scientific Survey. The UN agency that's conducting the terraforming experiment."

"So?"

The councilor sighed in exasperation. "Do you really need me to spell this out for you, Lane?"

"Humor me."

"It's no secret that of all the agencies and corporations vying for a slice of the new *open* Mars, MASS are the most powerful. When the AsterX agreement ends next week, they will be in an even greater position of power. Some feel that AsterX would have much to gain by discrediting them, particularly technologically."

Lane sat with his arms folded, studying the water flowing from the fountain. "Interesting theory, but utter nonsense."

"I agree. But, there you go. I just wanted to bring you up to speed."

Lane let a moment pass before replying, "Thanks. I appreciate it."

They sat contemplating this while the little bird

returned, or maybe a different one of the same species. It had a friend with it this time.

"You know, I never really saw the merit in giving such carte blanche over the exploration of Mars to MASS," said Lane finally.

Yuto shrugged. "They're a UN agency. Non-profit, multi-country. They represent Earth's interests. They've been here purely for the scientific study. The search for life is important to humanity. Anyway, we had no choice, you know that. It was the concession we had to make to get access to nuclear technology. Without that reactor spitting out the watts over in the Industrial Sector, none of this would be possible."

Lane snapped, "I've made no secret of my objections to their ever expanding mandate. When they first came here, it was supposedly about the search for life. That's fine, let them do it. But no sooner than they put the first bootprint on the surface, they were already drafting up a list of no-go areas. Places with valuable mineral resources that we can't access. All because of the perceived fear of biological contamination."

"It's a valid concern."

"True, but why do I get the feeling they were just doing it to undermine AsterX, and ultimately the prosperity of Mars?"

"You can't say AsterX hasn't grown rich and fat from your ten year exclusive agreement."

Lane smiled reluctantly. "No, I can't." He looked around and leaned in. "But their mandate has changed yet again, to this terraforming experiment. I mean... what the hell is that about?"

"I don't know, but it's quite exciting. You know the idea was originally postulated back in the early part of the twenty-first century. Using a nuclear detonation at the poles to convert the frozen CO_2 into a greenhouse gas. And as we all know, enough of that in the atmosphere and the planet starts to warm up."

"It's an interesting idea, and has a modicum of scientific credibility. But to actually make a difference you would need a continuous chain of detonations, hundreds, maybe even thousands. What they're planning is to test a single thermonuclear device. It seems utterly pointless to me."

Yuto smiled. "Do I detect a hint of envy there?"

Lane laughed. "I just think it's a complete and utter waste of resources."

"It's Earth's money, so what do we care? Anyway, it's just an experiment. To test the theory."

Lane folded his arms. "Maybe it will prove worthwhile, but somehow I doubt it."

"Well it's going to make a spectacular finale to the decennial celebrations. They plan to detonate it at the end, with the whole event relayed to the big screen we're erecting on the Avenue, via their orbital space station. Everyone's looking forward to it."

They stopped their conversation as a G2 unit rolled by. The birds that had been cleaning their wings in the fountain flew off and the unit stopped and started poking around in the flowerbeds. Yuto removed a slate from his pocket and tapped a few icons. The G2 unit spun around and moved off. When it had disappeared from view around a corner of dense foliage, they continued their conversation.

"I know we've gone off topic a bit, so just one thing you need to be aware of. The courier that died was a Pioneer."

"One of the clones, yeah I heard."

Yuto shifted in his seat. "They don't like to be called that, Lane. They can be very touchy about it."

Lane nodded.

"The death of any colonist casts a dark shadow over all of us. It reminds us just how dangerous a place it is we live in. But the death of a Pioneer is doubly disturbing, after all they have been through to put us on the map, so to speak. So there are certain elements within the council who will not let this go."

Lane nodded again. "I get it. Watch my back."

"They'll be agitating for reduced compensation and minimal contracts to AsterX after the deadline."

Lane watched the birds fly off again, contemplating the current situation. He had lobbied hard to keep as many as possible of the lucrative contracts that they, AsterX, had built up over the last decade on Mars. As a reward for helping the fledgling colony gain its independence from Earth they had secured exclusive rights for mining on the planet and as a transit point en route to the asteroid belt, where the true riches lay. They had established a spaceport, shipyards, and a new base on Ceres. And Yuto was right, they had grown rich and fat on the proceeds. But in less than a week this exclusivity would be over and Mars would open up to everybody and anybody who had the wherewithal to mount such an operation. *All good things come to an end eventually,* he said to himself. It didn't help his cause, or that of AsterX, that his power base on the council had been eroded. The old guard: Dr. Malbec, Langthorp, Xenon, and others were now sidelined by the new young guns. Fresh with new ideas about how things should be run. His efforts to cultivate some of the new blood had had mixed results. The best of these was Yuto, and Lane didn't trust him with anything more than minor affairs. He was too much of a political animal; you were never quite sure what side, if any, he was on.

But Lane still had friends among the Pioneers. A group of around a hundred that had *been* the colony before independence. They almost all had positions in administration. They were the hands and feet on the ground, they kept the wheels of the colony moving on a sol-to-sol basis. But they were clannish and almost tribal in their allegiances. Probably since most of them were clones, created during the colony's dark past. They were literally a breed apart and that made them tricky to deal with. But their power was waning, and with Mars now taking in a hundred new people on average every six months, it wouldn't be long before they too became a relic of the past.

Nevertheless, there was now a clone dead in suspicious circumstances. What did it mean? What concerned Lane was not the fact that there were elements within the Mars council using this as a weapon against him, he had expected as much. No, what bothered him was a Pioneer, working as a courier for MASS. That was unusual in itself. The fact that his rover exploded as it did just added more intrigue to the riddle. What's more, MASS had so far refused to let the rover be inspected by anybody but themselves. It smelled all wrong to Lane. Something was going on, something different. Something that didn't quite fit.

He shook his head and rose from the stone plinth by the fountain. He cast his gaze around the splendor of the biodome, and marveled at what had been achieved over the last decade up here. But his time, and that of AsterX would soon be over. *Out with the old in with the new,* he said to himself. He sighed. *my work is done, time to move on.* He bid Yuto goodbye and walked out of the biodome.

6

AT THE RED ROCK

The meeting with Dr. Malbec left Mia feeling out of sorts. She was going places in her thoughts that she didn't want to go. All the old crap that she had tried to bury was swimming around her head when she finally arrived back at her accommodation pod.

Strictly speaking, she still had another two hours of work tasks before clocking off, but since Dr. Malbec had seen fit to clear her slate, Mia decided to take advantage of the extra free time and go back home where she could feel sorry for herself in comfort.

She was surprised to find the door to the pod that she shared with Christian Smithson, her boyfriend of two months, unlocked and ajar. Mia hesitated before going in, a reflex action honed from her time on the force. A front door that was supposed to be closed but wasn't was seldom a good sign. She instinctively reached to her hip, where her service pistol would have been, back in the day. But of course it wasn't there. She felt a bit of a fool at the reflex. She was being stupid. It must have been the conversation with Dr. Malbec that got her all jumpy.

Nevertheless, she stood to the side, gently opened the door wide with one hand, and peered in. She could hear someone moving around, so she entered slowly, her body on high alert. On the bed was a black holdall. Mia didn't remember leaving that there this morning. Standing beside it was a tall man dressed in the standard issue colony flight suit. It was Christian, her boyfriend. But she hadn't expected him back from Elysium for another week.

Mia relaxed and rushed in to greet him. "Chris, you're back."

He spun around and a look of shock rippled across his face momentarily. 'Mia... eh... it's you... eh, I thought you'd still be at work."

This felt to Mia more like an accusation than a greeting. "Yeah, well I got the rest of the sol off, it's a long story." She went to embrace him, but it seemed a little lackluster.

"So, what happened? How come you're here, I thought you'd gone for another week at least."

"Eh... something cropped up."

Mia looked down at the holdall. "Here, let me give you a hand unpacking."

His hand lifted to stop her. "No, it's okay."

She looked at him for a moment and then her eyes

went to the holdall. He wasn't unpacking it, he was packing. She looked around the tiny pod and realized that he had removed all his stuff. She turned back to him. "What's going on, Chris?"

He shrugged and looked down. "Eh..." He scratched his chin and looked around at nothing in particular.

"Chris, tell me."

"Mia... eh... we've had a great time together, really great I mean."

"Had?"

"Yeah, I've had a blast... but..."

Here it comes, thought Mia. She didn't need a diploma to figure it out, she was being dumped. *Bastard.*

"But, I've been thinking, and, you know, I'm not sure I'm ready for this... just yet."

"Ready for what?" Screw it, she'd make him work for it.

"Us, I mean." His shoulders drooped, and he spat out, "I'm not ready to get into a long term thing... and I don't want to be holding you back, you know."

"So, it's not me, it's you. Is that it?"

He face lit up. "Yes, exactly. I'm so glad you understand. You're so cool, Mia. I'll always have a special place in my heart for you."

Mia said nothing. What was there to say? She just stood there and watched as he packed the last of his stuff into the holdall, all the time muttering away about how he had had a great time but now it was time to move on. She watched him from a place far far away. She only returned when he kissed her on the cheek and walked out the door.

Mia sat on the edge of the bed and put her face in her hands. How could she not have seen this coming? After a while, sitting there, she realized she really didn't care that much about him going. What she did care about, was the manner in which he went. *Was he really just going to disappear and not tell her?*

They met shortly after Mia arrived on the planet. He was a courier working for MASS, so he was away most of the time, particularly if he was going on a trip to Elysium—that was a ten sol round trip. But when he was here in Jezero City they had spent most of their time together. And since the terms of Mia's sponsorship provided her with her own accommodation pod, he had moved out of the dorms for MASS contractors, and in with her. Now where was he going? Back to the dorms, maybe over to the Industrial Sector? *To hell with him*, she thought.

Mia really wanted someone to talk to, but she realized that she had fallen into the trap of spending so much time with Chris, she had neglected to foster any other relationships. *Well that's going to change*, she decided, *right now*. She wasn't going to mope. Far from it. She would grab a shower, put on a clean kit, head out to the Avenue, and celebrate her newfound freedom.

By the time she stepped out of her tiny shower and got dressed she was already feeling better. Mia checked her appearance in the mirror, and when she satisfied herself that she probably wouldn't scare any small children she reached for her jewelry box. It was gone.

For a moment she did a mental double take. *It must be here.* She searched all the places it should be, then all the places where it could be, followed by all the places that were simply wishful thinking. There weren't that many places to search. It didn't take long for Mia to accept it was gone. *He must have taken it.* She would have to find him and get it back—and then beat the crap out of him.

It was a frantic two hours later when Mia finally plonked her ass down on a barstool in the Red Rock Cafe on the Avenue. She picked a quiet corner, she was very pissed off.

"Bad day at the office?" Victor Wanyama, the resident barman came over and wiped the counter in front of her.

"Men are complete bastards." Mia scowled.

"I'll try not to take that personally."

She looked up at him and sighed. "Okay, let me refine that. Just the ones I get involved with."

"Ah... what a relief, for a moment there you had me worried. Boyfriend trouble?"

"Yeah, the bastard dumped me and then robbed me."

"Ouch."

"So I could use a drink."

"Certainly madam, only right and proper, what'll it be?"

"Do you still have that synthetic bourbon?"

"You're in luck, we have a fresh batch just in from the labs, and this distillation is only mildly radioactive."

"Hit me then."

Mia put back a shot and felt the edge coming off her rage. Victor poured her another. "So, did you manage to get your stuff back?"

"No. He had taken the rover over to the Industrial Sector before I could catch up with him. I was too late, and I can't go after him either, don't have the clearance."

"Did you report it?"

Mia looked up at him. "To who? There's no 911 here. I can't call and get a SWAT team sent after him."

"Central?" offered Victor.

"Pen pushing middle managers, they're useless."

"Actually they don't use pens, this is a very hi-tech environment, don't you know." He poured her another drink. "Anyway, every cloud has a silver lining."

"Oh yeah. How so?"

"Well, you and I are now free to mate and do our bit for population growth."

Mia laughed. "I'd love to, only problem is I've decided to take a vow of celibacy—sorry." She made a sad face.

"Damn, there go all my hopes and dreams."

Mia laughed again. "Stop, Victor. You're making me laugh. This is not what I need right now. I want to be miserable in comfort."

But before Victor could continue the jousting he had to move off to serve others, and Mia was left with her thoughts. She realized that after all that had happened to her today she was emotionally exhausted. It wasn't anger so much as frustration. The fact was that she let people just ride all over her—yet again, and there was nothing she could do about it.

Victor returned. "Another shot?"

Mia put her hand over the glass. "No. I'm good here. Thanks."

"Sure."

"Hey Victor. How long have you been here?"

"Five years next month."

"So you must know, what do people do when they have a problem?"

"Depends on the problem."

"Well, I just got something that means a lot to me stolen, and it seems like there's nothing I can do about it, nowhere to go."

Victor looked around and leaned over. "Look Mia." His voice was low. "I know a few people, you know, they help sort out... issues."

"You mean like a bunch of heavies."

"Things have grown fast here, Mia, we don't have all the official infrastructure you'd expect. So we improvise."

"I just find it odd that there isn't a department in Central that deals with these things."

"We did have a few lawyers a while back. But we put them outside with no EVA suits to see if they could talk themselves out of dying. Mars won."

Mia laughed, downed the last of her drink and slid off

the barstool. "Thanks for the drink, and thanks for the offer, but I'll figure something out myself."

"No worries." Victor saluted her.

As Mia walked back to her pod, she began to think there might just be a way for her to track down Christian and get her stuff back. But it would mean reopening old wounds. Could she go there? Did it really mean that much to her to risk facing those demons again? *Best I sleep on it. See how I feel in the morning.*

7

G2 UNIT

Mia stood on the opposite side of the holo-table from Dr. Malbec and the eccentric G2 unit, Gizmo. She had made up her mind earlier that morning, partly because she knew if she ever wanted to see her stuff again, then this was the only way. Take Malbec up on her offer and on the side, she could track down Christian and confront him.

But there was another reason. She was not going to let herself be a doormat anymore. The last time she had, it ruined her life. But it was the conversation with Victor at The Red Rock that had begun to resonate with her—the realization that there was no one she could turn to for help. So she made her decision, dive in and face down her demons, for better or for worse. Mia made the call, and within thirty minutes she was back in Dr. Malbec's lair getting up to speed.

Above the surface of the holo-table a 3D rendering of

the Nili Fossae trench ballooned out before them. This was a region some two hundred kilometers northwest of Jezero Crater, where the unfortunate courier had met his end. It was the droid that was currently doing the explaining to Mia. Something she had difficulty following as she had never experienced a G2 unit with almost sentient abilities.

"This is the location of the mining facility." The droid pointed about halfway up a long deep gouge in the Martian surface. "This is the MASS research station further up here," it continued.

Mia took a moment to digest all the information and to realign to the reality that she was talking to a droid. "So where did the rover blow up?"

The 3D topographical rendering spun and zoomed in on an area far to the south of the mine. A red dot pulsed on the exact location. "Here."

"And what's that?"

"That's a way station." It was Malbec that answered. "The mine is too far to travel in one sol, so we have these way stations at various points along the route. That way people can get some food and rest, and refuel."

"Like a Martian truck stop?" said Mia.

"Exactly." Malbec zoomed out on the rendering and Mia could see Jezero Crater. "The route to this mine follows an ancient riverbed out of the crater here. You can see it twists and turns—it's an arduous journey. That's why this way station was put here, just before heading into the Nili Fossae trench."

Jezero City

"So what was he doing up there?"

"We understand he was doing a resupply mission to the MASS research station."

"We understand? You mean you're not sure what he was doing?"

"Jay Eriksen was an original colonist, a Pioneer..."

"You mean he was one of the clones?"

Malbec stiffened. "We don't call them that. They... they're a little touchy about it."

"Okay, gotcha. Don't call them clones. Anyway, so what if he was a clo... I mean a Pioneer."

"Nothing, really. Just that he was contracting to MASS as a courier."

This made no sense to Mia. She was beginning to think that this might have been a bad idea. She really had no clue as to how this place operated. "You're gonna have to explain that one."

"The Mars Alliance Scientific Survey, MASS, is a UN agency set up about seven years ago to do research on the planet. Their primary objective is to look for life. But over the years that has expanded to encompass a whole range of experiments and research."

"They're the ones doing the nuke experiment up north?" Mia pointed at the ceiling.

"Yes. Among other things."

"And?" Mia prompted.

"And, well, they operate semi-autonomously. They answer to the UN back on Earth. We don't have a lot of control over them."

"Ahh... I'm beginning to see the picture. So let me take a guess at the scene here. There's a bunch of guys, that you have no control over, running around on the planet doing whatever they like. I can imagine that a lot of the old guard here don't like that."

Dr. Malbec nodded.

"So it's a bit strange that one of the *Pioneers* decided to work for them," Mia continued.

"Very strange."

"Okay, assuming your hunch is correct and he was murdered, that would mean every one of the other Pioneers would be a suspect, including you, Dr. Malbec."

Mia could see she was taken aback by that. "Eh... I see your reasoning, but I don't think so."

"Look, Jann. I know this is probably not what you want to hear, but most murders are done by someone known to the victim. Someone who held a grudge, a jilted lover—it's all very predictable. So, first we look at all the ex girlfriends or boyfriends, all the people who may have been pissed off with him for whatever reason. In other words, the usual suspects."

Malbec said nothing, just pursed her lips.

"Do we have any forensics?" she continued.

"Eh..."

Mia rolled her eyes. "I thought you guys were at the pinnacle of human technology. You must have something!"

"Well that's the thing. We don't have access to the

rover, it belongs to MASS. They have what's left of it over at their sector."

"So, what about the body?"

"They haven't released it yet."

"Can they do that?"

"For a while. They have the right under the UN/Mars agreement to conduct their own investigation first."

"And you think they're hiding something?"

"That is my fear." Dr. Malbec switched off the holotable and walked to the window. She stared out for a moment before turning back to Mia. "I want you to find out what it is."

Mia moved next to her and looked out at the domed skyline of Jezero City. "So what you really want is for me to spy for you."

"Something's going on, Mia. Something that they don't want us to know about. Something that could jeopardize our future here. So, yes. I want you to do some snooping around and find out what you can. We can set you up as a courier. That means you'll have access to anywhere you want to go. No one around here bats an eye at couriers, they keep the whole place operating. So you won't be noticed. Nobody knows you, you're just a regular colonist, fresh off the ship."

Mia let out a big long sigh. This was getting serious. Doing routine police work, following up leads was one thing, but now Malbec wanted her to go dig up something to put flesh on the bones of her paranoid imaginings. She sighed again. Still, being able to go wherever she wanted meant she could track down Chris and kick his balls. She could do a bit of snooping for Malbec, keep her happy. "Okay. But there's a problem. I can't drive a rover."

Malbec's face was serious, but she nodded. "Thank you, Mia. And the rover is no problem. Gizmo can operate it for you."

"What. Me?" The outburst from the little robot jolted Mia into remembering it was still there.

"Yes, Gizmo." Jann turned back to Mia. "All couriers travel with a G2 unit. We can make Gizmo here look more like one of them. He can be my eyes and ears and you'll also find him incredibly useful."

"A G2 unit? I won't do it. I will not allow myself to be humiliated like this." Gizmo twitched and shuddered.

Mia's jaw dropped. Was she really hearing this? What the hell was inside that machine?"

"I'm sorry, Gizmo. But you know this is extremely important to me, and the whole colony. I wouldn't ask you if there were any other way."

Why was Malbec reasoning with this robot, like it was some child that needed to be humored? Mia felt like giving it a kick and telling it to get on with it.

"Well, if you insist. But I'm not going to enjoy it," said Gizmo.

Screw this, thought Mia. "Look, if it's all the same to you, Dr. Malbec, a standard G2 unit is fine by me."

"No. As you can probably tell, Gizmo's capabilities go way beyond a standard unit."

"By several order of magnitude," the droid added.

"He'll keep you safe. God knows, he's saved my ass more than once."

"Do I have to give up my plasma weapons?" Gizmo raised an arm and from its shoulder a serious looking gun muzzle telescoped out.

"We can talk about that later," said Jann.

Mia looked at the droid. It seemed to be appraising her at the same time. *What the hell am I getting myself into here?*

8

NILI FOSSAE

As soon as Mia had agreed to undertake the investigation, Dr. Malbec and her associates wasted no time in preparing the necessary identity she would require. As this was being set in motion, Mia also didn't waste time bringing Dr. Jann Malbec up to speed on the necessity of simple investigative procedure.

"Police work," she explained, "is ninety percent procedure: doing the forensics, interviewing people and asking a lot of questions. There's very little glamour involved, it's mainly a long slow slog. Some people liken it to flying an airplane. Hours of boredom sandwiched between a few minutes of sheer terror."

It was with this line of reasoning that Mia suggested the best place to start was by paying a visit to the scene of the alleged crime. The item on her agenda after that, would be to seek out the location of what remained of the rover, and the body of Jay Eriksen. How she would, or even could, do this was still to be established. So later that day, under the guise of a courier delivering supplies to the way station at Nili Fossae, Mia and her G2 unit set out from Jezero City in a newly commandeered rover.

It bounced and rocked its way along the central valley as the road twisted and turned, following the topography that had been laid down millennia ago by the course of the ancient river. This route had been reshaped even further by the constant movement of human activity, as machines made their way from Jezero City up to the mining outpost and research stations. Mia glanced out the windscreen at a distinctly homemade road sign that had been hammered into the hard ground at the side of the road. It was a crudely shaped arrow tied to a post, on which someone had hand painted Nili Fossae.

Gizmo was currently at the wheel, although there was no wheel, as such. As far as Mia could ascertain, the rover was controlled by a joystick. Not that Gizmo was even using it. The robot seemed to be plugged in somehow, a direct interface, so to speak. It had also been stripped of various appendages that had been deemed incompatible with its new role as a disguised G2 unit. What function the missing pieces performed for the droid, Mia had no idea. But it was clear to her that Gizmo was very unhappy about their loss. The concept of being in such close proximity to a malcontented sentient droid was one that Mia was still struggling to get her head around.

"So, how come you're so smart, Gizmo?"

"Relative to what?"

Mia already regretted asking the question, but since it would take hours to reach the site of the rover explosion she was looking for a way to break the monotony of the journey.

"Other G2 units. I mean they're all pretty dumb service droids."

"Their cognitive abilities are self contained and limited to the processing power that is engineered into the unit itself. My mind, if you wish to call it that, resides primarily in the Jezero City mainframe."

"So why don't they build the other units like you?"

"It would require too much processing power to sustain a larger number and it is unnecessary, as they have a very rudimentary instruction set that can easily be accommodated within the unit."

"I still don't see why more of you weren't built since you seem, well, quite extraordinary."

Gizmo's head swiveled to focus directly on Mia, who was sitting in the passenger seat beside it. She was taken aback at the sudden movement from the droid.

"Shouldn't you be, like, looking at the road while you're driving?" She waved a hand in the general direction they were traveling.

"I *am* looking at the road, as you put it. I'm also correlating several simultaneous input streams giving me data on position, velocity, and topography, as well as anticipating course corrections and adjustments based on upcoming terrain anomalies. On top of that I am also monitoring a multitude of other extraneous processes that have no direct influence on our current exercise. I shall not bore you with explaining any of these, as most would be beyond your comprehension."

"Sorry I mentioned it," was the best she could manage to reply. After that, she decided to keep quiet, as the conversation, if you could call it that, was proving more frustrating than entertaining.

AFTER A WHILE MIA noticed the landscape was beginning to change. They were higher up now, moving out of the narrow channel near Jezero. The sides of the gorge flattened out and they were entering a high, wide plateau. The road here was less defined and recognizable only because of the innumerable tire tracks in the dry dusty regolith. Boredom was getting the better of Mia, so she decided to continue her interrogation of the droid.

"So who built you?"

"I was designed and built by Nills Langthorp."

"The clone?"

Gizmo swiveled its head to look at her again.

"What? What did I say now?" Mia sighed.

"They do not like being called that. Pioneer is the preferred nomenclature."

"Right, fine, okay, Pioneer then."

Gizmo reoriented its head. "I was initially designed as a service and maintenance droid, but my fundamental cognitive reasoning was based on advanced neural network structures. This was so I could evolve to manage all the life support systems in the colony. At that time my creator, Nills Langthorp, was the only human living in the colony and he wanted a backup system, in case he became incapacitated in some way."

"So you can control all the life support systems?"

"Not anymore. My access to those higher level systems was curtailed as the colony grew. And there were also those that were fearful of allowing a semi-sentient droid to have that much control."

"In case you decided you didn't like humans and turned off all the air?"

"Precisely."

Mia was beginning to understand why the powers that be in the colony were not inclined to build any more robots with the level of sophistication that Gizmo possessed. Too resource hungry and just plain too dangerous to have around. She wondered if this droid's sols were numbered.

Over the next few hours Mia gleaned as much information as she could from the little robot. It seemed to know everything about the colony, all the way back to well before independence from Earth. She found it fascinating partly because of the subject matter and partly because Gizmo seemed very responsive to all her questions. Even if, at times, she got more than a hint of intellectual arrogance. It was deep into an explanation of the various zones housed within the Industrial Sector of the colony when it stopped talking and brought the rover to a halt. It looked over at Mia.

"What? What's wrong?'

"We are here. This is where the courier Jay Eriksen died."

"Okay then, let's saddle up and take a look."

Mia was glad of the distraction. The journey had been long and arduous and she had a new admiration for the colonists who worked as couriers. It had seemed to her, and those working in the agri-domes, like such a glamorous occupation. But after several hours inside a rover traversing the surface of Mars she realized it took a special type of person to do it.

She booted up her EVA suit and snapped on the helmet. She had only gone EVA three times before, for very short periods. This would be her first time going solo. She instinctively took a deep breath before closing her visor. Then she let it out and took another deep breath. So far so good. She headed for the airlock.

When the door opened, and Mia stepped out onto the surface, a wave of exhilaration rippled through her. She had not expected this. So wrapped up had she been with the politics and intrigue of the mission that she had forgotten to consider the realities. It was the same feeling she had had stepping off the transit craft that very first sol after she had arrived on Mars. But back then they were all ferried into transportation. Now she felt more like a genuine colonist.

She was snapped out of her thoughts by Gizmo's

voice in her headset. "This way, follow me." The droid moved past her, its sleek tracks making easy work of the terrain. It had parked the rover a little off the roadway to make room for any of the gigantic ore-carriers that might be coming down from the mines. Mia began to take in her surroundings as they moved. They were on a vast and relatively flat plateau. Ahead of her to the north, mountains rose up and she could see the wide gap in the line that signified the entrance to the Nili Fossae trench, a six hundred kilometer long gouge in the Martian surface. Mia could make out the silhouette of the way station to the north, its large solar array glinting in the late evening sunlight as the panels tracked around to follow it.

"This is the place." Gizmo's voice in Mia's headset.

She stopped and looked around. There was not much to see. All signs of the explosion had been ground out of existence by the pummeling of ore-carriers crossing back and forth along this road. She moved off to widen her search. The little robot tagged along. In reality Mia was not expecting to find anything. But that, in of itself, said something. It said that MASS had done a very good job of cleaning up all traces of the accident.

"If you tell me what you are looking for, perhaps I can assist in the search," the droid offered.

Mia looked down at Gizmo. "I'm not sure. Can you detect metal?"

"Absolutely. Would you like me to scan the area for debris from the explosion?"

"You can do that?"

"Yes, of course."

"Okay, that would be great. I'm going to take a walk along this road. Up to where the body was found."

Gizmo spun around and Mia assumed it had begun its search, so she started walking. Jay Eriksen's body had been found approximately five hundred meters from the site of the explosion. Mia paced this out and looked around. He was still alive when the rover exploded so he must have gotten out before it went boom. *Why did he do that?* she wondered. She looked up and could just make out the vague shape of the way station. How far away it must have seemed to Eriksen as he fought his way towards it, his air running out. *I wonder when he knew he wouldn't make it?*

After a short while Mia returned to find Gizmo still moving around the site. "Anything?"

"Nothing."

"Nothing at all, not even a washer?"

"Nothing."

"How is that possible?"

"I would suggest that MASS were using the same, or better, technology than I am to do a thorough clean up."

"Why would they do that?"

"Because they could?" offered Gizmo.

"Or because they didn't want anything to be found."

"Not even a washer," confirmed the droid.

"Why would that be?"

"I am reluctant to admit it, but I have no reasonable answer."

Mia took one last look around. "Well, I think we're done here. Let's get back to the rover and move on to the way station."

Her plan had been to spend the night in the way station. She had checked the schedules of other couriers and reckoned there was a good chance that somebody else might be holed up there tonight. Somebody she could possibly pump for information, maybe get a better understanding on what went on up here. As luck would have it, when they arrived, Mia could see one of the massive ore-carriers already attached to the umbilical carousel. This enabled people and goods to be moved in and out of the way station completely in an atmosphere. It reminded Mia of the passenger walkways in large airports that bring you directly onto the aircraft without having to walk out on the apron. On the side of the massive truck was emblazoned the AsterX logo. "We're in luck, Gizmo. Looks like there's at least one other person here."

"Forgive my ignorance, but how can that be construed as *luck*?"

She looked at the little robot. "Gizmo, keep in mind that they'll probably have their own G2 unit with them. So you need to drop the fancypants talk and keep up the pretense that you are an ordinary dumb droid, okay?"

"Okay, if you insist. But I'm not going to enjoy it."

"If it makes you feel any better, this is not about enjoyment. We're here to work, and that means pumping this guy, assuming it is a guy, for information."

"Very well, but I can't imagine that a humble ore hauler will have anything useful between his ears."

"Because if you want to know what's happening on the street, you start talking to a local. Get it?"

"No. There are no streets here."

Mia contemplated the little droid for a moment. "Has anyone told you you can be a serious pain in the ass?"

"On many occasions."

Mia sighed and pointed out the windscreen. "Come on, just take us in."

The dominant structure of the way station was a large dome, perhaps thirty meters across, constructed from the same cement material used for every other structure on Mars. It was that same rough-hewn rust color that made it seem almost part of the landscape. It reminded Mia of some ancient adobe building from some long forgotten civilization. Radiating out of the central building were several smaller domes designed for storage, power and a methane reactor. Behind that was a large solar array mounted on stilts, tracking the sun. Snaking out from the main dome was a long tunnel with airlocks dotted along its side. Gizmo reversed the rover up to one of these and they connected to the umbilical with a satisfying clunk.

Mia moved out of the rover and into the tunnel walkway. As she walked, lights automatically came on to illuminate the area. Gizmo shut down the rover and followed along behind. The tunnel finally opened out directly into the main dome. At the far end a man sat at a table, eating. He lifted his head up for a moment as Mia and Gizmo entered, gave a vague nod as a greeting, then went straight back to his food.

Mia reckoned that this guy didn't look like a talker. It would take a bit of work to pry him open.

"Greetings, Earthling." Gizmo waved.

Oh shit, Mia groaned to herself.

The guy stopped mid chew and stared at the droid with his mouth open. Even the G2 unit at his side swiveled its head around to investigate.

Mia laughed nervously. "Eh... just ignore him, he's... eh... a new model. Takes a bit of getting used to."

"He?" Said the guy.

Mia laughed again. "It's a long story. I'll tell you some other time."

This explanation seemed to satisfy him as he shook his head. "Weird droid." And went back to eating. Mia kept moving, hoping to make it to the accommodation module without any more drama.

This was a much smaller dome connected to the main dome by a short tunnel. It had six sleeping pods, three on either side of a dividing wall that bisected the space. She saw the red *occupied* sign on the hatch of one of the pods, and assumed this was where the guy eating must have bagged. She went to the other side and commandeered a pod. It was tiny, just enough room for her and Gizmo to squeeze in. She sat on the edge of the bed and turned to it.

"Is there some part of *act like a dumb G2 robot* you don't understand?"

"My apologies, it just slipped out."

"The whole point is not to draw too much attention to ourselves. Otherwise people will get suspicious and I'll get nothing out of them. Okay?"

"I understand. I will endeavor to be as dumb as possible from now on."

Mia spent some time getting moved in and cleaned up, partly because she needed to and partly because it would be the normal behavior of a courier after a long day cooped up in a supply rover. She sent Gizmo off to unload the supplies with strict instructions not to speak to anyone, or anything, for that matter. Now she was ready to tackle the driver of the AsterX ore-carrier.

When Mia returned to the main rest area, he was still there, looking at something on his slate. He glanced over at her, she nodded a hello. He reciprocated and went back to his slate. She headed for the galley and loaded up a tray with what looked to be a chicken curry and a fruit juice, then brought it over to his table.

"Mind if I join you? First sol on the job, still finding my feet."

He looked up and hesitated, then gestured at the seat opposite, "Sure, go ahead."

Mia sat down diagonally across from him, so as not to be too in his face, give him some room. "I assume that gigantic machine is yours. Must be a challenge driving that."

He cocked an eyebrow in her direction. "You get used to it after a while."

"Been doing it long?" Mia was pushing it now, taking a risk. He could easily not reply or give her a monosyllabic answer. He put his slate down, looked at her for a moment and started talking.

"Two years on the ore-carriers, three more driving rovers before that."

"Wow, so you must have been all over the planet."

"Most places. I've been over to Elysium I don't know how many times."

"What's that like?" Mia was busy shoveling chicken curry into herself. She'd not realized how hungry she was.

"It's a very long journey. Nearly two thousand kilometers. It's a ten sol round trip." Then he got into his stride. "But it's very flat, not like this route. Once you get out of Jezero and into Isidis, it's wide open space all the way to the foothills of Elysium Mons."

Mia responded with her best wide-eyed rookie look, enthralled by the knowledge of the wise old master.

"I'm surprised they gave you this route first. It can be very tricky." He began to relax.

"Yeah, I had a bit of concern, considering what happened to that guy a few days ago." Mia wondered if he would take the bait.

He did. "Poor bastard." He paused for a moment, then leaned in and spoke in a low voice. "You know he was one of the clones?"

Mia decided it might be better if she hadn't known this fact. "No, I didn't."

"Yep, weird. I mean, what's a clone doing working as a courier?"

"They don't normally do that?"

"No. Why would they? They run the place up here so, yeah, it's a bit strange."

"Maybe he just wanted to take in some of the scenery?"

He grunted. "Maybe. But why work for MASS? I mean they hate those guys."

"Really?" Mia's eyes widened.

He sat back and considered her. "You don't know much, do you?"

Mia gave her best rookie shrug. "No, I've only been here a few months."

"And they let you be a courier on the Nili Fossae route? Jezero, they must be scraping the barrel. Eh... no offense."

"It's okay. None taken." Mia let some time pass in silence as she cleaned her plate. "So, what do you think happened with the rover?" She tried to get the conversation back on track.

He lazily shrugged his shoulders. "Hard to say. They don't tell me shit around here. But what I heard was the fuel tank exploded. Just one of those things. He got out, apparently, but his suit was too badly damaged to make it back here. You have to feel sorry for him, even if he was a clone. I mean, all they want to do is go back to Earth."

This was news to Mia. "Earth?"

"Yeah, it's all they ever talk about—well, some of them."

"And this guy, did he want to go back?"

"I didn't know him that well, only met him a few times—here, actually. Last time I saw him he was sitting where you are now, going on and on about how he was going back to Earth. Which is complete bullshit, considering they're forbidden from going."

"Really?" Now Mia was getting very interested. "Why not?"

"Jeez, lady, you really are just off the boat. You're clueless."

But before Mia could perform another one of her best *oh great and wise master, please enlighten me* looks, Gizmo whizzed in and stationed itself beside the table.

"I have transported and made secure all provisions from the supply rover. How may I now best facilitate in unburdening you from need and want?"

The guy let out a long guttural laugh and slapped the table. "They really stuck it to you good with that one. That must be the dumbest G2 unit I've ever heard." He leaned across the table to Mia. "Listen, here's a piece of advice. Take that unit back and tell them you want one of these standard units." He waved in the direction of his own unit. "Totally reliable, never gives any bother." He looked at Gizmo. "This one's a complete dud—big time."

"Thank you," said Mia. "I'll be sure to mention it to them when I get back."

At that, he stood up. "It's getting late. Time for me to hit the sack." He reached over to Mia with an outstretched hand. "Good talking to you. Might catch you again, on down the trail."

"Yeah. Goodnight."

He left with his G2 unit in tow. When she was sure he was out of earshot she glared at Gizmo.

"What? said the little droid. "What did I say wrong now?"

Mia fought her exasperation. "It's okay, Gizmo. Never mind."

"It appears that my act has been very convincing."

"Yeah, but not quite the way I had in mind." Mia began digesting some of what the ore hauler had said.

"Gizmo, tell me what you know about the... eh, Pioneers. And why they want to go back to Earth so badly."

9

DISTRACTION

Dr. Jann Malbec stood looking at the broad expanse of the Jezero Crater from her living quarters high above the city skyline. She had been watching a new colonist ship coming in to land at the spaceport. She always found it fascinating to watch these gigantic ships slowly maneuver their way from orbit to a vertical landing, shrouded in a vast plume of dust as they touched down. Onboard would be nearly a hundred people: new colonists, contractors, tourists and a cohort of representatives from various Earthbound corporations that were here to cement their new concessions ahead of the decennial celebrations. Over the next few weeks this same ship would be refueled and resupplied and would lift off again with a much smaller passenger manifest back to Earth. Her musing was broken by a pinging sound from her slate. She fished it out of a pocket in her robe and tapped an icon.

"Just letting you know, the council session is starting in fifteen minutes." It was Werren, her aide.

"Thanks, I'll head down shortly." She put the slate back in her pocket and took one last look towards the spaceport. The plume of dust had settled just enough that she could make out the upper section of the giant ship standing proud in the morning sun, like a twenty-first century monument to humanity's scientific greatness. She turned away and made for the lift.

IN THE CENTRAL dais of the bio-dome many of the councilors and aides had already assembled. Some were seated while others congregated in knots of conversation, gathering like-minded political positions. They were the old guard, of which Jann was one, comprised mainly of Pioneers and others from the time before Martian independence. In fact, many of them were instrumental in achieving this autonomy. Then there was a grouping that was generally described as the new guard. These were mainly colonists that had arrived over the last decade, as well as representatives of MASS. They had new ideas and new visions for the development of the colony. For a long time the balance of power lay with the old guard, but they had been losing ground for some time, and that loss of influence had been gaining traction as they approached the decennial celebrations.

But Jann was okay with that—mostly. She had never been someone who desired power, it had been thrust upon her by virtue of her exploits, not by any political maneuvering on her part. She also understood the need for change. What she and her compatriots had done to forge the colony out of the chaos of corporate manipulation, fiscal greed and the pre-revolutionary genetic experimentation, had been to create this very situation. One where the foundation was laid down for the next generation to have a stable, normalized, cohesive environment—free from extraneous influences.

But all change brings with it an equal measure of uncertainty. As the hour neared when the exclusive rights granted to Lane Zebos and the AsterX mining company would come to an end. New Earthbound corporations were lobbying hard to be included in the next round. These had all found more sympathetic ears with the new guard than that of the old, who were reluctant to change and happy to maintain the status quo. But now the new generation of power brokers were in the ascendance. They knew their time was coming, and soon.

In this mix was MASS, a UN agency granted rights to conduct scientific studies of Mars. Their odd, semi-autonomous mandate came about from Earth's exploitation of Mars's need for energy. Shortly after independence it became evident to the then council, that to expand they were going to need more than just solar panels. Nuclear power was the obvious choice but this meant kowtowing to the UN on Earth, many of whom were still angry at having been forced, as they saw it, to grant independence to the colonists on Mars. This same cohort now saw their opportunity to row back on that agreement. A torturous negotiation ensued with neither side looking like backing down. But in the end, a compromise was reached.

It was agreed that a new, non-profit, UN agency would be set up to have oversight of all nuclear projects on Mars. In return this agency would be granted full and unrestricted access to the planet and its moons for the purposes of scientific investigation, the primary objective being the search for life. They would also be allowed seats on the Council of Mars, with full voting rights.

So began the rise of MASS as both an industrial and political power. With the decline of the old guard and the new young guns not yet fully formed, MASS had reached a point that saw them control the balance of power.

Jann scanned the assembled gathering looking for Nills. He promised her he would be here, but she couldn't see him anywhere yet.

"Where's Nills?" She turned to her aide.

"He's running a bit late."

"Ahh... Dr. Malbec." Robb Hoburg sidled over and offered a hand. "Looking as youthful as ever."

"Thank you. The wonders of modern science."

"Speaking of science, our erstwhile MASS colleagues are treating us all to a detailed explanation of their terraforming experiment."

"Interesting."

"Well, I for one am ready to kill myself now rather than suffer through another science lecture." Robb rolled his eyes.

"Yes, they do love their science. Almost as much as they love themselves."

"Now, now, Dr. Malbec. Cynicism is best left to those of us who are old and tired, like my good self."

"Not too old and tired that you can't fight for the cause anymore I trust."

"Ahh... I fear our sol draws near, Jann. That time when we are made redundant and put out to pasture."

"Well, we still need to get through these decennial celebrations first. After that I think your prophecy might be accurate." Jann glanced at a small knot of councilors huddled together in hushed conversation. "I see Yuto has acquired some new friends."

"Yes, the Mazen Corporation. They're here, like all the others, to lobby for access rights. Be prepared for a request for your vote."

"Why so, do they not have enough?"

"It seems they have fallen out of favor with MASS, so may need a backup plan."

"And you, Robb. How are you voting?"

"You know me, Jann. I have a simple rule. Anyone MASS takes a dislike to I regard as fine upstanding citizens."

"Good to know. I'll keep that in mind for the future."

"You're assuming you and I have a future."

Jann considered this to be an odd remark for the old

councilor. True, he seemed tired and cynical lately. But he was not a fatalist. This was new. What was also new was the presence of the AsterX CEO, Lane Zebos. It was rare that he showed up in person, generally leaving such formalities to one of his minions. Perhaps he too was putting on a show of defiance in the face of the seismic changes that were about to occur. Of all the stakeholders, AsterX was the one who would lose the most, now that their exclusive contract was expiring. The chime sounded, signaling all present to take their seats so the session could begin. Jann moved towards her place, nodding her acknowledgment to those who wished to catch her eye before kickoff.

THE PRELIMINARIES PASSED QUICKLY, as they always did, and then it was on to a number of issues requiring a vote by show of hands. But none were contentious so this too passed without incident. Once the business of decision was concluded the council finally moved on to the meat of the session, which was the agenda item labeled *any other business*. If there were snakes in the grass this was generally where they would show up. Jann nodded to Robb Hoburg, who stood and took the floor.

"Councilor Hoburg has the floor," said the Chair, formally signaling that Robb could speak his piece without interruption.

He cleared his throat. "With regard to the unfortunate death of Jay Eriksen, a longstanding and esteemed citizen of the colony, I wish to inquire of MASS as to the specific nature of this tragic accident." He sat down.

Evon Dent, the most senior director of the Mars Alliance Scientific Survey stood. "I would like to take this opportunity to express our sadness at the loss of such an upstanding and committed colonist. We will all feel his loss. His body was released this morning in preparation for his interment in the colony mausoleum."

"Duly noted. But can you enlighten the council as to the manner of his death?" Robb prompted.

"We have not concluded our investigations but initial indications would seem to suggest that the fuel tank on the rover was faulty, which caused it to rupture and subsequently ignite. The result was a catastrophic loss of rover integrity."

"You mean it blew up?" said Robb.

"That is our general conclusion."

"And do you know what caused this?" Robb continued.

"We are still investigating it, but our initial findings indicate a fault was introduced during the last full service on the rover, conducted, I might add, by the AsterX maintenance team."

"That's horseshit." Lane Zebos stood. "Show me the evidence."

"I'm afraid the rover was too badly damaged," said Evon.

"Hand it over to us then, if you can't find anything.

We'll get to the bottom of it." Lane was getting more animated.

"I'm sorry, but this is being viewed as an internal matter for MASS."

"More horseshit. This is a colony matter, you can't just keep us out of it."

"Agreed. The colony will be updated in due course once our investigations are concluded. But it is up to the council whether they share this information with AsterX, especially considering your rights are soon to expire."

"What are you hiding, Evon? What game are you up to?"

"That's enough, Mr. Zebos." The Chair rapped hard with his gavel. "This is not the time nor place to cast irresponsible accusations. You are disrespecting the decorum of this council."

Lane scowled, sat down, and glanced at Jann.

The Chair continued, "That said, Mr. Zebos does have a point, in that this is a colony issue. The death of a colonist makes it so, but the death of a Pioneer makes it doubly so. This cuts us deeply and as such this unfortunate incident needs to be brought to a satisfactory conclusion. So with that in mind, when will your investigation be completed and a report drawn up?"

Evon Dent stood again. "Unfortunately, with all the preparations for the decennial celebration, not to mention the complex work involved in getting the terraforming experiment ready on time, I'm afraid we are a little stretched. my understanding is we should be finished shortly after the big event."

"Very well. We will expect this report at next month's council session." The Chair rapped once with his gavel to signal that this piece of business was concluded. There were a few moments silence as the Chair looked around at the assembled council to see if anyone else had something new to discuss. "If there are no other items, then we can move on to the more joyous business of the decennial celebrations. Councilor Mika, I believe you have a report on progress?"

Mika stood and began her report. It consisted mainly of a list of resource allocations, timetables and schedules, but eventually she got into the event itself. It was to be held in the Central Avenue in Jezero City, as this was the only common space big enough to accommodate everyone. All citizens were required to be present, and transportation would be provided to ship them in from all sectors of the colony. A skeleton staff would remain at those installations that could not be left unattended, such as the main life support centers and areas in the Industrial Sector, even at the mines of Nili Fossae and Elysium. Since all these people were contractors working directly for the colony, or for AsterX or MASS, they were not citizens of Mars and were not required to be present.

The event itself would take place over a sol, starting early afternoon with light entertainment, followed by a documentary on the formation of the colony. After that, food would be served, followed by formal speeches and prerecorded messages of goodwill from various heads of state on Earth. The finale was to be a speech by none other than Xenon Hybrid, President of Mars, whereupon he would ceremoniously countdown to the moment when the MASS terraforming event at the North Pole would be detonated. This would be observed directly from the MASS space station in orbit and relayed to the assembled colonists on the giant screen that had been erected for the occasion. It was certain to be a spectacular event, signifying a new phase in the development of the colony. After that everybody would probably get drunk.

ALTHOUGH THE TERRAFORMING event was without doubt the most anticipated element of the entire celebration, there was also considerable interest and chatter about Xenon Hybrid actually turning up and doing the honors. The reason for that was that most of the current colonists, save for the Pioneers, had never seen the President. In fact, most surmised that he was a mythical figure that didn't really exist, someone the Pioneers made up just to sound even more weird and mysterious than they already were. So, for Xenon to show up and make a speech would be an event in and of itself.

But he was very real. He had been created during the genetic experimentation that constituted the pre-revolution colony, back in the days of its dark past. Not a clone, as such, but an augmented aggregation of several human DNA sequences. He was in essence, an entirely new species of human, homo-ares as opposed to homo-sapiens. In many respects he was the only true Martian. Around thirty of this new species had been created at the time, however all but Xenon had died. He was the last. In the early years he had been greatly used and abused like his brethren, as tools of the geneticists. But after the revolution, his worldview coalesced with that of the other colonists, as he realized that they were all in this together. And so he came to be one of the heroes of the battle for independence.

But it was his superior intellect and almost Zen like demeanor that led the colonists to choose him as president of the newly created planet state of Mars. This title carried no power, it was purely ceremonial. So after a while, Xenon resigned from the council and took to more cerebral activities, such as compiling a history of the colony. It was during this period that he announced one sol that he was *going native*.

So enthralled had he become in the myth and history of Mars that, in his mind, the only way to fully attain the level of understanding he aspired to was to go deeper, to touch the soul of the planet. So he packed a modified rover with provisions and headed out to explore. That was three Earth years ago, and he had only been back once since. Not voluntarily, but because his rover broke down somewhere west of Gale Crater and had to be evacuated. But as soon as a new rover was made ready he was off again. His extraordinary journey took him to many far-flung corners of the planet which, in the beginning, he documented diligently. Soon though, he decided that these simple observations were insufficient, and so began a period of essay writing and later, philosophical musings. His most recent output had taken the form of poetry, some of which he had planned to recite at the celebrations.

There were those, of course, that complained about the precious colony resources that were required to maintain this perceived insanity. Xenon had to be resupplied on a regular basis out in the field, as he refused to return until, as he put it, his internal philosophical dialogues had been concluded. An entire department in Central was dedicated solely to this.

But others argued that every great civilization had its thinkers, poets and philosophers—and if Xenon wished to dedicate this period of his life to considering the true essence of the Martian sunrise, then good on him. He was elevating the colony to something more than a simple amalgam of industry and commerce. He was defining the very essence of a new Martian civilization. They considered him an invaluable cultural project and signed off on the budgets for it, without question, every term. The fact that he would be the one to count down to the terraforming event and herald this new phase in the advancement of the colony was also symbolically significant. He had even written a poem about it, which he would recite before the detonation.

. . .

COUNCILOR MIKA HORI sat down after she had brought the council up to speed on how the preparations were proceeding. This left only one other item of business, and that was a short lecture by MASS on the science behind their terraforming event. The Chair tapped his gavel once again and signaled for Evon Dent to proceed. Evon stood up and tapped an icon on his desk screen. The holo-table in the center of the table blossomed to life with a photo-realistic 3D rendering of the planet Earth. It rotated slowly.

"Earth," he began. "A world where water flows freely on two-thirds of the surface. A world rich in vegetation, made possible by the cycle of evaporation and precipitation."

The Earth continued to rotate for a moment before fading out and being replaced by the planet Mars.

"Another world where water is plentiful. But here of course, it is too cold to exist as a liquid. But what if we could warm the planet, enough for the ice and permafrost to melt?"

"Then Jezero Crater would fill up again and we would all drown," said Yuto, accompanied by a ripple of laughter.

"True, but you don't need worry just yet," said Evon with a chuckle. "We're a long way from achieving that. What we're doing is an experiment to test the theory, nothing more. Anyway, as I was saying, how could we go about warming up the planet?" The rotating orb switched to Earth again.

"Well, as a species, we have plenty of experience in warming up planets. By introducing CO_2 into the atmosphere more of the sun's energy is trapped, unable to escape back out into space, and the planet starts to warm." The 3D image changed back again to Mars. This time it zoomed in on the North Pole.

"As it happens, there is a great deal of CO_2 on Mars, frozen at the poles. If we could somehow release this into the atmosphere, then we could make a start warming up the planet. But before any of this can be attempted in earnest, a few numbers need to be established. So, to help us start understanding the necessary equations we are going to detonate a small thermonuclear fission device."

The rotating Mars rendering zoomed in to a location north of the 60 degree latitude, near the pole.

"The event will vaporize a significant quantity of frozen CO_2 and release it into the atmosphere. From this we can ascertain any resultant temperature deviation with measurements that will be made over the next year. While the experiment itself will do nothing to actually terraform the planet, it will give us the quantity of new CO_2 introduced, the resultant rise in temperature and also the energy requirement to create these numbers. From that we can then calculate the required volume of CO_2 and the total amount of energy it would take to raise the planet's temperature to a point where water could flow freely again on Mars."

A simulation played, showing the planet warming, water flowing and the dusty red desert turning to green.

"That's complete horseshit," said Zebos. "There just isn't enough CO_2 on Mars to do it, and you would need the entire arsenal of Earth's nukes, by a factor of ten, to make any headway at all."

Evon sighed. "That may well be the case, Mr. Zebos. But without this experiment we are completely in the dark as to the feasibility. Once we execute this we'll have some empirical data to work with."

"Well, I think it's a wonderful idea and it's going to make a spectacular finale to our celebrations." Yuto chimed in.

"But what about radiation?" Councilor Mika looked concerned.

"It's many thousands of kilometers away, nothing to fear. Also, here on Mars we have the advantage that everything is hardened against many forms of radiation." He chuckled. "So, I think we're pretty safe."

Jann had heard enough. Since the formal business of the council had been concluded before Evon's lecture any were free to leave if they chose. So she stood up, thanked the Chair, her fellow councilors and Evon Dent in the correct diplomatic order, and turned to go. But as she did she made deliberate eye contact with Lane Zebos. She moved away from the council dais and into the surrounding biodome gardens, heading for her favorite spot. It was far enough from the council area so as not to hear anything, but also secluded so that no one could overhear any conversation within. She sat down on a stone plinth and listened to the gently cascading water in the fountain. She didn't need to wait long before Lane Zebos came strolling in and sat down beside her.

"So, Lane, what brings you to a council session? Normally you just send a minion."

"Ah... one last meeting, for old times sake."

"The end of an era, then?"

"I wouldn't quite say the end. But certainly the beginning of the end. It will still take the vultures time to pick clean what we've created here."

"Well, you've still managed to retain quite a few concessions. You're still an important part of the colony, and will be for a long time to come."

Lane sighed. "Yeah, I suppose you're right."

"So why all the *horseshit*, were you trying to bait Evon Dent?"

Lane laughed. "Ah... no, not really. I'm not a politician, I can't do subterfuge, I have to say it as I see it."

They let a moment pass before Lane continued, "I've heard a rumor."

Jann looked at him. "Go on."

"It seems that quite a number of councilors are siding with MASS in trying to pin the blame for that accident on us."

"Hardly a rumor, Lane. I think that was fairly obvious from the meeting."

"I don't mean we messed up technically, but that we deliberately sabotaged the rover."

"And why would you do that?

Lane looked intensely at Jann. "I'm sure you can have a guess."

"I can, but I want to hear it from you."

Lane shook his head. "To turn more of the Pioneers against MASS? If one of their number died in a sloppy accident in a MASS rover, that would not go down well."

"And what would that do, ultimately?"

Lane shifted. "I thought you were on our side. You don't actually believe any of this... horseshit, do you?"

Jann folded her hands in her lap. "No, Lane. Like you I consider it complete... equine excrement."

Lane settled down. "Thank you. For a moment there I thought we had lost you to the dark side, too." He paused. "So what do you think they're up to?"

"Distraction," said Jann matter of factly.

"I've no idea what that means, you'll need to give me more to work with."

"Here's what's going to happen, Lane. When MASS provide their report it will show it was caused by something outside anyone's control. It will be put down to just one of those unfortunate things that happen every now and again. AsterX will be exonerated, not your fault after all, and that will be that."

Lane looked over at Jann. "How do you know that?"

"It's the oldest trick in the book, Lane. If you don't want something scrutinized then you create a distraction. The more outrageous the better. Everybody starts jumping up and down, looking in the wrong place. So when MASS put this down to an unfortunate accident, everybody accepts it because they're too busy arguing over whether AsterX was involved or not. It's a sleight of hand. It's what magicians have been doing for millennia. Create a distraction to distract the audience while the trick is played out behind everyone's back."

Lane shrugged. "I still don't get it. Why would they do that? Why go to all that trouble?"

"Like I said, so that the trick isn't seen."

"But what trick... wait a minute... are you saying they did this themselves, that it wasn't an accident?"

"No, I'm not saying that. At least not without any evidence. I'm curious about what game, if any, they're playing."

They sat in silence for a while. Lane stared at the fountain. "Would be nice if we could pick through the remains of that rover they have locked away."

"What would you look for if you could?"

"Oh... try and see where the main destruction occurred, do some analysis of the components to look for stress, for failure, maybe do some chemical analysis and look for traces of explosives or other foreign compounds." He regarded Jann again. "But that's not going to happen. They have it locked down tight, no way to examine it."

"What if there was a way for someone to get in, someone not technical, what would they look for?"

This time Lane studied Jann's face for a moment and a smile began to break across his face. "Don't tell me you got someone on the inside?"

Jann shrugged. "It's purely a hypothetical question, a *what if*."

"Well, one could take a lot of photographs of the damaged areas, close ups of the various parts. Also any components they might have removed and put aside, even how those are arranged could give us a clue as to what they might be looking for. And since we're speaking *hypothetically*, it would be even better to acquire one or two of these components and do some chemical analysis. In a *hypothetically* independent lab, of course."

"I see. Very interesting."

Lane favored her with a broad smile. "You've become a wily old fox, Jann. Back in the day you would skewer your enemies in the eye with that spear you used to carry."

Jann laughed. "Yes, but we've moved on a lot since then. Nobody wants to go back to those times."

In the corner of her eye she spotted two of Zebos' minions walking toward them. Lane had also seen them coming and nodded to them. They stopped and waited at a respectful distance, not wishing to intrude, content that they had been acknowledged.

Lane stood up. "Looks like I have to go."

Jann also stood and Lane threw his arms around her in a firm hug. He broke away, holding one of her hands in both of his. "Let's not leave it so long the next time. Maybe when all these celebrations are over you and Nills will pay us a visit up at the space station."

"Yes, perhaps. We haven't been up there in a while."

He shook her hand again and turned to go, but took only a few steps before he turned back. "Just one other thing. The EVA suit."

"What do you mean?"

"It would be interesting to have a closer look at the EVA suit the courier was wearing. Considering what you were saying about distractions. Everyone is talking about the rover. Nobody has mentioned the EVA suit."

"I'll keep that in mind."

"Anyway, just a thought. Gotta go." He turned and walked away.

10

CENTRAL LOGISTICS

Mia woke late the next morning to find the ore hauler she had talked to the previous night was long gone. She was disappointed, as she would have liked to pump him a bit more. But the way station was deserted now, so it was time to move on. She had considered heading up to the mining outpost deeper into the Nili Fossae gorge, then traveling on to the MASS research station about fifty kilometers further north. But that all changed when she received a message from Central Logistics, informing her that she should make her way back to HQ and await her next assignment as a courier. This was the department that controlled and managed all movements of goods and people around the sectors of the colony and its satellite installations. Since, strictly speaking, she was in the employ of Central Logistics, Mia was not surprised by this directive, but she did have a sense that Dr. Malbec might be behind it. So, Mia and Gizmo spent the early morning prepping the rover for its return journey, filling its tanks with oxygen and methane, swapping out scrubbers, loading it up with waste for recycling and doing a full systems check. Once done, Mia squandered no time in starting out on the long journey back to Jezero. If nothing else, it would give her time to think and digest what she had learned so far.

HER CONVERSATION with the ore hauler the previous night had thrown up some interesting information. Nothing specific, just some noisy data. The courier had been a clone, that much she had already known. But what had also piqued her interest was why this guy had such a desire to return to Earth, and why this was forbidden for clones.

It was not an issue for the colonists, nor for the contractors working for AsterX or MASS. In fact, if a colonist was not happy or not performing well, or even if they were just plain troublemakers, they would be shipped back at the first opportunity. But this was obviously something denied to the clones. At first Mia was annoyed at missing out on an opportunity to quiz the ore hauler further about it when Gizmo had interrupted them and stuck its big metal foot in it. But after spending a few hours talking to Gizmo on the long journey back, she was rather glad it did.

Mia probed the droid for information on the history

of the clones as well as the UN agency involved in the Mars scientific survey, and had become so enthralled by how much it knew that she lost track of time. Two things about Gizmo began to fascinate her. One was its depth of knowledge. She'd had no idea it possessed such an encyclopedic reservoir of information on the colony, all the way back to when the first bootprint was stamped onto the surface. The second thing that fascinated her was the fact that it regurgitated this information without bias of any sort. It had no opinion, no agenda, no social or religious allegiance. What it gave her was pure data. From Mia's perspective it was the perfect witness. So, from what the little robot was telling her, and from what she had known herself, she pieced together a history of the Pioneers—the clones.

The first humans to populate Mars came on a one-way ticket. There was no going back, they were here to stay. This suicidal colonization project was funded by a kind of reality TV franchise. Surprisingly, it worked for a while. That was until the population of Earth got bored and the money started to run out. So a new source of funding was sought and this turned out to center around setting up a genetic research lab, for doing research that was ethically forbidden on Earth, namely human experimentation. This did not go well, as a rogue genetically modified bacterium escaped into the colony environment, infecting the colonist population with an incurable psychotic malaise. Most died during this period. But then it got even weirder, as the stored DNA of these, now dead, colonists was used to create the clones. The Pioneers.

Mia had been aware of the rogue bacterium, as it had made its way back to Earth and started to infect the population there. She vaguely remembered that a way to kill it was found quickly so its effects were minimal. All that happened shortly before Mars had gained its independence. But what Gizmo was telling her seemed to have taken place long before any of this.

"But if all this happened almost twenty years ago, like you say, Gizmo, then how come all the clones look like they're thirty-five?"

"Grow tanks."

"Grow tanks?"

"It was a technology developed whereby the original DNA could be utilized as a biological blueprint to reconstitute an exact human replica from a stem cell biomass. This process was accelerated so that the resultant being was, to all intents and purposes, fully grown."

"Holy crap."

"Indeed."

"So why the hangup over Earth, why can't they go back?"

"A side effect, if you will, of this process was retained memory essence. In simple terms, many could remember significant elements of their previous incarnation. In one way this was fortunate as they still possessed the skills of the original. An ethical problem arose after the colony came back online and was no longer conducting clandestine experiments. This was a result of the families of the original colonists, after presuming their loved ones were dead, discovered exact replicas of their loved ones existed as a result of experimenting on the colonists."

"Yes, I can see how that would go down."

"So, once the clones had regained control of the colony they made a pact to never return to Earth. They would stay true to the ideals of the first colonists. Hence the reason they prefer the title Pioneers."

"That's quite a story. How come this isn't more widely known? I mean, this is the first time I've heard it."

"It is all there if you choose to look deep enough. But they do not talk about it much, and it is never mentioned in any public profiles of the colony."

All this new information was fermenting in Mia's head as they made their way down the ancient riverbed and into Jezero crater. The terrain eventually flattened out and about half a kilometer into the crater the road forked. The right would lead them to Jezero City, but Gizmo took the left fork. This would take them to the Industrial Sector and the location of Central Logistics HQ.

The Industrial Sector was situated approximately thirty kilometers north of Jezero City on the far side of the crater. The very first colonists had discovered an extensive cave system with a small entrance at the base of the crater rim. It was mineral rich so, over time, they sealed up the entrance with a massive airlock, created an atmosphere inside and began to mine it. But it had a dark past as the clandestine location of most of the genetic experiments that had taken place here. After the demise of the geneticists, the outpost went through a period of decline as essential maintenance resources from Earth became scarce. At one point the colonists had considered abandoning it and consolidating at what was now called Jezero City. But it was independence and the collaboration with the asteroid mining corporation, AsterX, that had breathed new life into it.

As a reward for their assistance in helping the fledgling colony state gain independence from Earth, AsterX had been granted exclusive rights to use Mars as a waypoint en route to the exploration and exploitation of the mineral resources of the Asteroid Belt. All the extracted ore was returned to Mars and processed in the refineries of the Industrial Sector before being shipped back to Earth. This was the main economic engine that financed the colony and enabled it to prosper greatly.

The old cave system had been expanded enormously since then, with new additions to the existing facility spreading out across the surface of the crater. There were shipyards, for the building and servicing of all manner of craft that plied the trade routes from Earth, Ceres and the Asteroid Belt. Around these shipyards were small factories that processed the raw materials that fed the expanding colony's insatiable needs. Regolith from Nili Fossae was processed into the cement that fed the large scale 3D printers that worked 24.5/7 building the vision.

Ore from Elysium ended up as steel and aluminum, rolled into sheets or extruded into the myriad of shapes needed by the designers of the ever more complex structures. Sand and silicas were transformed into glass and ceramics. Chemical reactors produced methane, oxygen, hydrogen and a raft of other gasses by the ton. It was a busy place.

Entrenched in this hive of industry was Central Logistics. Its sole purpose was to distribute goods throughout the entire colony and its satellite outposts. Raw materials from the Industrial Sector, food from the agri-domes in Jezero City, specialist supplies from Earth, water from the processing plants out at Isidis, ore from the mines. As well as provisioning the multitude of way stations and outlying research stations. All of this required a small army of couriers and vehicles to haul goods from A to B. From the big ore-carriers to specialist containers for transporting liquids and gases, to pressurized rovers for transporting food and other perishable goods that could not withstand the rigors of a 0.6% atmospheric pressure and outside temperatures of minus sixty.

Gizmo backed the rover into a free docking station connecting them to the main hub at Logistics. That same instant the screen in the rover dash lit up as the central mainframe communicated with it, assessing its systems and resources, and scheduling the next tasks for the crew.

Mia read the screen. They were to unload the spent supplies brought back from the way station and take them to the reprocessing center. That would be Gizmo's job. *Good,* she thought, that will keep it out of trouble for a while. Mia, on the other hand, was to report to Central to pick up a package for delivery to the MASS HQ. *Excellent, looks like Dr. Malbec found me a way in.* HQ was where the remains of the wrecked rover was stored, so delivering there would at least get her moving in the right direction with the minimum amount of suspicion. The problem was the MASS sector was a sizable facility, and Mia still did not know the exact location of the rover's remains. And even if she did, she would still have to find a way to get past security.

The pick up wasn't for another hour. The rover needed to be fueled and given the once over. This was done automatically but still took time. So Mia decided to head for the canteen. She was hungry, and she also hoped she might get an opportunity to talk to a few other couriers.

"Now remember, Gizmo, try and act like a dumb G2 unit. We're in the hornet's nest here, okay?"

"I shall do my best, difficult as that may be."

"And take your time doing this unloading. I don't want you hanging around me in the canteen."

"I sense I am being shunned."

Mia raised a finger to the robot, like a teacher making a point to an errant child. "Be good, okay?"

"Define good?"

"Oh for heavens sake, Gizmo, just... don't communicate with anyone."

"If you insist."

"I do. Now, I'll let you get on with it. I'm going to eat."

THE CANTEEN WAS SPACIOUS. It was early evening and the main shift of the sol was over. Half a dozen couriers were milling around, some eating, some just chatting. Mia headed to the food dispensing machines and placed her palm on the ID pad. It scanned her hand and then displayed her name along with a mug shot, and gave her the green light to make her selection. She grabbed a few energy bars, an apple, and a carton of juice, then turned around to decide where to sit. She was keen on not drawing too much attention to herself, to blend in with the ebb and flow of the crowd. The tables were in long rows with enough seating at each for around a dozen people. She picked an empty one and sat down in the middle. It didn't take long for someone to bring their tray over and sit down opposite her.

"Hi, haven't seen you around here before." He was a tall frizzy haired guy with an easy smile and a bright face. He reached over and offered his hand. "Dexter."

"Mia," she shook his hand. "Yeah, I'm new. Just started a few sols ago."

He looked around and gestured with both arms. "Welcome to courier central, where the great problems of the universe are discussed, and sometimes even solved." He touched a finger to the side of his nose.

Mia smiled back. "Good to know."

"So what route have they started you on?"

"I'm just back from delivering supplies to the way station at Nili Fossae."

Dexter's eyes widened. "Really? They don't normally give such a challenging journey to rookies. It took me three months before they let me out of the crater."

Mia decided it was best not to comment on it. Instead she changed direction and tried to get him talking about himself. "So you must have been everywhere by now?"

"Oh yes. I've done the Elysium route several times, even been up at the MASS research station in Utopia Planitia."

"What do they do up there... at the research station?"

"I don't know, something to do with the nuke experiment."

"Is that where they're doing it?"

"No, I don't think so. I heard it was further north, near the ice cap."

"That must be quite a journey."

"It's a bit boring, to be honest. Lots of flat featureless land. The only thing to break up the horizon are the way stations, and boy are they a happy sight after seven hours of traveling across nothing but flat emptiness."

Before Mia could think of a reply, another woman sat down beside Dexter with a flourish. She leaned across the table. "A word of warning," she jerked a thumb at him. "Our resident Romeo. He hits on all the new girls."

Dexter rolled his eyes. "Jeez Marina, thanks. Now why you have to go and say that, eh?"

Marina laughed and slapped him on the back, then tipped her head at Mia. "Just joking, he's really dead on, got a girl over at Jezero he's really sweet on."

Mia could see Dexter was taking umbrage. "Yes, I do, thank you Marina." He turned to Mia and jerked a thumb back. "Mother Superior is what we call Marina around here. Mainly on account of her advanced years." He tapped his head. "Going a bit senile."

They bounced off each other in this vein for a while and Mia zoned out. When they finally settled down into what passed for rational conversation between this pair, Mia decided to venture a question.

"Do either of you know Christian Smithson?" There was sudden silence. A definite reaction. One that signaled to Mia that, A: they did know Chris. And B: they didn't much care for him.

Marina looked around the canteen and then leaned in. "How well do you know Christian?"

Mia considered this for a moment. "Well, judging by your reaction, not very well. He's an ex boyfriend. He dumped me a while back, which is fine by me. But he ran off with some stuff that I'd rather like to get back."

Marina sat back. "You poor baby, how'd you get mixed up with that shit?"

Mia shrugged.

"Well, you're better off without him, take my word on that. And you're not the only one he's robbed either."

"So where is he?" Mia asked.

"You just missed him. He headed out on a run for MASS this morning, won't be back for a few sols."

Damn it, Mia thought. But before she could quiz them any more her slate pinged. She fished it out of her pocket, and read a message from Gizmo.

I have completed my allotted tasks and have elected to seek refuge, in solitude I might add, within the confines of the rover, as it seems I am not to be trusted in public. By the way, in case you have not checked in, there is a package waiting for you at Central.

Mia shook her head.

"Problem?" asked Dexter.

"No, just some droid issues, no biggie." She shoved the slate back in her pocket and stood up. "Gotta go, nice talking to you all."

They said their goodbyes, and Mia headed for Central.

11

DUMB DROID

The package was small, about the size of a box of chocolates, well-wrapped and marked Top Priority. According to the instructions on the rover screen Mia had to deliver this, in person, to Lab-B13, which was located very close to the maintenance area in the MASS research sector.

It had all the hallmarks of Dr. Jann Malbec. A simple ruse to get Mia as close as possible to the location of the damaged rover, without raising any suspicion. That was the easy bit. The hard part would be finding the exact location when she got inside and then doing some investigating without being rumbled. But Mia had a pretty good idea how to do that from all her years of experience on the force. It was called acting dumb.

The facility was at the far end of the Industrial Sector, and then some. It was a large isolated cluster of domes connected to the main reactor via a half kilometer long tunnel. One got the feeling that MASS wanted to be as far away as humanly possible, but still have an escape route.

They followed the road that skirted the bulk of the sector, tracking along the rim on the crater wall. Further on, this road would lead out of Jezero heading east into the Isidis Plain, and then on to Elysium. But Mia and Gizmo weren't going that far, it took them around forty minutes to navigate their way around to the main entrance of the MASS facility and dock.

The rear airlock door of the rover opened and standing right inside the entrance was a guy with the bored look of someone who would rather not be here dealing with couriers.

"What you got for us?"

"Package for Lab-B13." She handed him her slate.

He glanced at it. "Okay, fine. I'll take it from here."

"Sorry, *top priority*. I need to deliver it personally, see." Mia showed him the line on the slate again.

"Yeah, whatever." He stood aside and let Mia and Gizmo, who was holding the package, into the facility.

"You're sure giving that droid a workout. Do you really need it to carry such a small box?"

"Ah... it's new, got to train it. You know how clunky these G2 units are when you first get them."

"Yeah, pretty dumb."

Mia was only a few paces down the corridor when he called out, "Hey, you know where you're going?"

"Yes, no problem. Thanks." She picked up the pace.

When they were out of earshot she turned to Gizmo. "There's a lot of cameras around here."

"Yes, I have noticed."

"Come on, let's get this delivered. Then we'll see if we can get lost in this maze."

It didn't take long to hand the package over to another bored looking lab tech. Mia realized then that this was generally how couriers were treated. Whether it was here on Mars or back on Earth. They were, for the most part, invisible to people. Nobody took any notice. She had to admit it was an elegantly brilliant way to move around incognito, except for the cameras. If someone got suspicious later, all they needed to do was go back through the recording and she'd be fingered. But at least the facility seemed to be devoid of people. The corridors were deserted.

"Listen, Gizmo. I want you to start acting strange."

"Some would say that is how I normally act."

"Yes, well that's not what I mean. What I want you to do is stop and start, then maybe spin around a few times, like your circuitry is acting up. Then stop. I'll start poking and prodding you, like I'm trying to fix you. I might even give you a kick."

"And the point of all this physical abuse?"

"I want to make it seem like you're on the blink, screwed up your internal map of the facility—so we look like we're lost."

"I have to admit, that is a reasonably good ruse, Mia."

"Thank you Gizmo. Now can you start going bonkers —for the cameras."

The little droid proceeded to stop and start, then it spun around a few times. Finally it went completely nuts, shaking and rocking with a ferocious pitch. Then it stopped for a brief second before racing off at high speed —towards the maintenance sector. Mia ran after it shouting, "Come back you dumb bucket of bolts!"

She found it at a junction. One way led back to the entrance, where they had come in. The other was where they wanted to go. She bent down and started poking and prodding and cursing it. Then she stood up and gave it a good hard kick. Gizmo sped off again, right into the maintenance sector. Mia fell over clutching her foot. Not because she was acting, more because it hurt like hell.

She managed to hobble down the corridor where Gizmo was now stationary. She whispered to it, "Where to now?"

"According to my calculations, the only section of this facility with an airlock big enough for a rover is on the other side of that door."

Mia walked over to where the little robot was facing. There was a small window in it about head height. She peered in. Right in the center of a small workshop were the remains of the vehicle. It looked like the carcass of some recently excavated dinosaur with wheels. Mia peered around the space. There was no one there.

"Come on, let's go." She cracked the door open and they moved inside.

"Gizmo, I trust you're recording all this."

"In 3D."

Mia looked down at Gizmo. "You can do that?"

"Only when I am not acting dumb."

THEY SPENT some time walking around the rover, examining it. The entire back was blown off. Three of its six wheels were also gone. From what Mia could see, a good deal of it had been dismantled. Three long tables held dozens of burnt and charred parts. Each was labeled with some alphanumeric code that she could not make out. She picked up a small component that looked like a plumbing valve, then extracted a clear plastic zip-lock bag, and dropped it in. She turned to Gizmo and held it up. "Exhibit A." Mia shoved it in her pocket.

She took one last look around. "Okay, I think we've done all we can here. Let's get out before we're spotted."

They were about to leave when Mia's attention was drawn to a door on what looked like a sealed room, like a spray booth in a car maintenance shop. She looked in through the window.

"Gizmo, quick. Over here."

She pointed. "The EVA suit. Let's check it out." Mia tried to open the door but it was locked. "Gizmo, do you think you could hack this?" She nodded at a keypad beside the door.

"My pleasure." The little droid proceeded to disassemble the unit with amazing dexterity. A few seconds later Mia heard a click, and the door swung open. She stepped in.

The suit looked dirty and battered, a large crack ran across the faceplate. "Looks like the poor guy lost all his air through this crack."

"Unlikely," said Gizmo.

"Why do you say that? I mean, he did die of asphyxiation."

"Correct. But I calculate a breach of this type would take approximately one hour and seventeen minutes to evacuate a fully resourced suit."

"Well maybe his power unit failed."

"Again, unlikely."

Mia asked, "How can you be sure?"

Gizmo reached up to the side of the suit, tapped some controls, and the suit lit up. Mia jumped back, startled. "Jeez, Gizmo. Warn me before you do that."

The robot interrogated the suit's systems. Mia looked at it for a few moments. "So you're saying he had little or no air to begin with."

Gizmo's head twitched. "That's interesting."

"What... what's interesting?"

"Very unusual."

"What, Gizmo?"

"He had less than seven percent oxygen reserve when he exited the rover. Someone had intentionally depleted it several hours earlier."

"How can you know all this, Gizmo?"

"It is tracked in the EVA suit's log."

Mia's brain tried to digest the ramifications of this revelation. Two things were clear to her. One was that Dr. Jann Malbec might not be as paranoid as Mia had originally thought. And the second was, they needed to get out of here as soon as possible.

"Say, what are you doing here? You're not supposed to be in this sector." Mia spun around to see the same guy that had met them at the airlock. He must have been monitoring the camera feeds. Maybe he wasn't as stupid as he looked.

"Oh... thank God you found us." Mia clutched at her chest. "I thought we'd have to stay the night here." She turned to Gizmo. "I don't know what's happened. My droid has gone bonkers. It must have blown a fuse or maybe it's having an existential crisis." She looked at the guy to see how all this was going down with him. He looked confused, but Mia could sense the same *whatever* attitude was beginning to get the upper hand. So she kicked Gizmo.

"Dumb robot lost its internal map! We've been wandering around trying to find our way out."

He moved over to take a closer look at Gizmo. "Yeah, some of the newer ones can be a bit sketchy. I haven't seen one like this before," he bent down to examine the droid.

Gizmo took off at high speed, out the door. Mia and

the guy chased after it. "See, I told you," panted Mia. "Totally nuts."

By the time they caught up with it, Gizmo was back at the entrance airlock of their rover. The guy stopped and had to lean against the wall to catch his breath.

"Well, would you look at that. It found it's way back after all." Mia turned around to see what he was doing. He was still getting it together.

"Sorry to put you to all this bother. I think I can manage from here." She backed towards the now open airlock. Gizmo was already inside.

"Hey... wait a minute." The guy had regained the use of his body and he was approaching her.

"Yes?" she said with a big smile.

"A bit of advice. Don't let them stick you with that droid, even if they fix it. It will be nothing but trouble. Make sure you get a different one."

"Sure... I'll remember that. Thanks." She turned back to Gizmo in the airlock, and gave it another kick. "Come on you dumb droid, let's get going."

12

SMOKING GUN

The lift door of Dr. Jann Malbec's living quarters opened with a ping and in stepped Nills Langthorp, to an immediate embrace. It took a few minutes for the pair to disentangle themselves.

"Miss me?" he said with a smile.

They embraced for a few more minutes.

"I'll take that as a yes."

"What took you so long? I was expecting you at the council meeting."

"Oh... the usual technical issues. It's not an easy job keeping the wheels of the Industrial Sector running like a Swiss watch."

They migrated to the large panoramic window. Nills sat down and looked out at the Jezero City skyline.

"I am really envious of the view you have here, Jann."

She sat down and poured two glasses of the best colony wine. She handed one to Nills.

"You can always move over here." She raised her glass.

Nills smiled. "Yeah, but who would keep the machines running over at Industrial?"

Jann looked wistful. "Sometimes I think you love your machines more than you do me."

Nills's face reconfigured into a dismayed expression. "That's absolutely not true. I love you both equally."

Jann threw a cushion at him, nearly spilling his wine. They laughed together.

"Speaking of machines, where's Gizmo?" Nills looked around.

"On a mission."

"What? You let him out on his own?"

"He's perfectly capable of looking after himself."

"But, Jann, we talked about this. It's not about Gizmo, it's about letting a semi-sentient robot, armed with plasma weapons, go wandering around. You know they're just waiting for an excuse to lobotomize him." He pointed in the direction of the council chamber.

"Relax, he's in disguise."

Nills sat back and took a long slow look at Jann. "Okay, what are you up to?"

Jann returned the look. "I found someone, unencumbered by any affiliation, to do some snooping around."

Nills remained silent and sipped his wine.

"She was an investigator back on Earth, so we set her

up as a courier and gave her Gizmo disguised as a G2 unit. And don't worry, we got rid of the weapons."

Nills said nothing as he digested this information. Finally he said, "How did Gizmo react to that?"

"Not very well. *I will not enjoy this.*" Jann put on her best Gizmo voice.

"Ha... it's nearly worth it to hear his reaction." Nills almost spat out his wine he was laughing so much. "So, you still think that rover accident was... not an accident?"

"Don't you?"

Nills put his glass down, sat back and looked out the window. "To be honest, I don't know what the heck is going on anymore. There was a time when you and I, and the others, knew every little detail of colony life. But now, we're no longer needed, or wanted. We're the past. The future of the colony is with the new blood."

"That doesn't mean we should sit back and ignore the potential threat to our world."

"No, no," he agreed. "You're right, it doesn't. But my point is still the same. I really don't know what's going on anymore."

Jann activated the tabletop screen. "Well here, maybe this will help you." She tapped an icon and a series of images slid open and arrayed themselves across the screen. Nills bent over to get a closer look. He touched an image, rotated and expanded it. He cocked an eyebrow at Jann.

"Where did you get these?"

"Mia and Gizmo. Our intrepid undercover team. She talked her way in to the MASS maintenance area."

"She's good, I'll give you that." Nills went back to studying the images.

"So what do you think?"

Nills scratched his chin as he examined an image of the rover carcass. "Massive explosion, probably the fuel tank. It opened up the rover like a can of beans in a microwave."

He flicked across a few more images. "I'll need to take a close look at these. Maybe get some clues as to why it blew up. But don't expect anything conclusive, it will just be speculation. It's a pity they won't allow us physical access to it so we could do our own investigation."

"Would this help?"

Nills looked over to see Jann holding up a clear plastic bag containing the charred remains of some component. He reached over and took it gently from her.

"You think you could do some forensics on it?"

"Looks like an oxygen regulator valve." He turned it over in his hand. "I suppose we could run a few tests on it, check for trace chemicals, that sort of thing. Not sure if it will tell us much, though."

"There's something else." Jann leaned in.

"Gizmo managed to access the EVA suit diagnostics. It turns out that when he escaped from the rover his suit was damaged, but not enough to prevent him making it to the way station. It seems that he had little or no air in the suit. It was hacked to make it look like it had a full tank.

Nills put the part down on the table. "Holy crap. Well that's a smoking gun if ever there was one."

"So you see, someone did try to kill him."

Nills shook his head in dismay and looked at Jann.

"So where is... Mia now?"

"Over at Central Logistics, talking to couriers, trying to get some clues as to the last movements of Jay Eriksen. It's the only way to get some idea of what he was up to, since we don't have access to the MASS database."

Nills flicked through some more photos. "You know, there *is* a way to find out what he was doing before the explosion."

"How?"

"The MASS database is restricted, so we can't get access to it. But Gizmo can. He can hack pretty much anything. But it would mean getting back into MASS HQ and finding a terminal. You think Mia could engineer that?"

"I'll run it by her."

"Just tell her to be real careful with Gizmo. If the council were to find out it's roaming around it will just give them an excuse to have it dismantled. They hate that robot."

"Don't worry, it will be fine."

13

MASS

Three hundred kilometers above the planet's surface, the MASS space station orbits the planet every one hundred and twelve minutes, passing directly over Jezero Crater and then tracking across both poles in turn. It is the central command for the survey mission, communicating once every orbital period with all assets on the ground.

The backbone of the station consists of a long skeletal truss section, terminating at one end with a plutonium-239 nuclear cryogenic propulsion system. This provides both the five thousand degree heat required to propel vaporized hydrogen out through the engines, and also electrical power for the entire station. Forward of this power plant is rigged a large diameter disk. At first glance this might look to be an effort to shield the rest of the station from the reactor core, and to some extent it performs this function. However, its main purpose is to house the secondary EMDrive system. A bizarre device, whose function is firmly rooted in the weirdness of quantum physics. Where the cryogenic propulsion system could trace its lineage back to the middle of the twentieth century, the EMDrive is very much a twenty-first century creation. Yet, compared to its older chemical cousin, it produces a feeble amount of thrust. Nonetheless, being electric it can run non-stop, and so can accelerate the spacecraft way beyond anything that a conventional rocket engine could hope to achieve. It is the engine of choice for all solar system craft, and the main reason that the colony on Mars, as well as the mining of the asteroid belt, could be accomplished.

Further along the station's central truss sits a constellation of tanks, wrapped around it like a bracelet. After these, the truss becomes sparse and skeletal, with nothing other than a few dish antennae to break up its visual continuity, until it finally terminates at a large spherical structure, comprised of several docking ports for transport craft. Currently two of these were occupied with small craft that made periodic commuter trips up and down to the planet's surface.

As impressive as all this engineering is, by far the most spectacular aspect of the station is the one hundred meter wide rotating torus, anchored just aft of the docking sphere. Its outer rim rotates at approximately three times a minute, giving its occupants a very comfortable Earthlike gravity. Along this rim are housed

Jezero City

all manner of labs, maintenance bays, conference rooms, recreation facilities and accommodations.

It was within one of the better appointed accommodation pods that Kane Butros, Second Director of the Mars Alliance Scientific Survey, was currently viewing a video recording of a very disgruntled colony courier giving a G2 unit a good kicking.

"Who else knows about this?" said Kane.

"I thought it would be better to keep it to ourselves, for the moment," said Blake Derringer, his security advisor.

"Good, keep it that way. I cannot stress enough how delicate the current situation is. A good deal of the MASS board are already spooked by this *rover accident*. We can't risk any further cause for suspicion." He looked back at the image of the courier on screen.

"So what the hell is going on here?"

"Apparently her G2 unit blew a fuse and they got lost while delivering a package to HQ."

"Well maybe they did?"

"I don't think so, have a look at this." Blake moved the video forward. Now on screen they could see both the courier and the robot inside the enclosure for the EVA suit. The robot seemed to be accessing the suit's diagnostics. The courier was talking.

"Any sound, can we hear what she's saying?"

"No, no sound, just video."

Kane scratched his chin and looked at his comrade. "Not good."

"My thoughts exactly," said Blake.

"Who is she?" He looked up. "And I mean who is she *really*, and who's put her up to this, and since when can a G2 unit run diagnostics on a EVA suit?"

"I already know who she is, and you're not going to like this. She's an ex-cop, came up here on sponsorship six months ago."

"A cop?"

"Ex-cop." Blake corrected.

"So who put her up to this? Someone has to be behind it."

"It's unclear. But let's face it, we both know who's been agitating for an investigation."

"Malbec?"

"Exactly. She's like a dog with a bone, won't let go."

"So she recruits some ex-cop colonist and all of a sudden we've got a problem." Kane was looking back at the frozen images on screen.

"The question is, how much can she find out between now and the event?"

"Even if Malbec does suspect something, the council are against her, she's powerless to influence anything." Kane waved a dismissive hand at his security advisor.

"Don't be so sure. From what I've heard of her reputation she's capable of anything. Underestimating Dr. Jann Malbec has been the downfall of many better than us."

"So what are you suggesting then, Blake?"

"Well, let's not be too hasty, we're so close now. We need to tread carefully."

"Well, I say we get rid of this cop… and that droid."

"I don't like it, too risky. We've already managed to load all the blame for the last *accident* onto AsterX, any further unexplained deaths would just raise more suspicion. Remember, Kane, I advised against the first operation."

"He had to go, you know that. There's no way we could let a clone go back to Earth. You knew that when we set him up."

"Still."

"Still nothing." Kane's tone became more measured, his stance aggressive. "Now is not the time to grow a conscience. You know what's at stake here, this needs to be dealt with, and soon."

His tone lightened and he moved to wrap an avuncular arm around the shoulder of his colleague. "You know, Blake, sometimes to get out of a problem, one needs to get into it more. Just remember, she's going to die anyway—they all are."

"True."

"Good. So we need to deal with this… *courier problem*, head on."

Blake nodded his approval.

"You'll need to go down there again and get this issue tidied up. And I need to keep the MASS board up here on track for the event. Already certain parties are spooked." He lowered his voice again. "There's talk of canceling."

"I know, I heard. But it's just talk."

"Maybe, but let's not give them any more excuses."

Kane looked back down at the screen as the video replayed. "So what else do we know about her?"

"Just what's in her official profile." Blake tapped an icon on the table screen and several documents appeared. Kane began to scan through them.

"One other thing, might be useful—then again, it might not. Her boyfriend is none other than Christian Smithson—and he just dumped her."

Kane lifted up his head and looked at his security advisor. "Interesting. But I can't see how that's going to help us."

"Maybe not. But the word is she's trying to track him down. Apparently he stole something from her, and she's desperate to get it back."

"Really? Maybe we've underestimated Christian. Speaking of which, where is he now?"

"In HQ, awaiting transport up here to the station. In fact it was he who brought this video to my attention."

"Do I detect an effort on his part to curry favor with us?"

"My thoughts exactly, considering he just shopped his ex-girlfriend."

"Hmmm... If that's the case, then I think we should keep him closer to us while this mission... plays out."

"I think it would be good to get him out of the way. However, we could let Mia Sorelli think he's actually holed up somewhere... isolated, but accessible."

"Ahhh... I see where you're going now, very good, that could work."

"She would try and head out there, she might even break a few rules along the way. Good opportunity for an accident."

Kane smiled. "A bit like our other friend."

"Exactly, and if we plan it right then we might be able to add more weight to AsterX's technical incompetence."

Kane thought for a moment. "Okay, do it. But get it done quick. We have a lot at stake here."

Blake nodded. "Consider it done."

14

HARSH ENVIRONMENT

Blake Derringer disliked being on the planet's surface, he found himself ill suited to the one-third gravity environment. These frustrations emanated mainly from the disruption it caused to his finely honed physical training schedule. All that he had trained his body to do seemed to be pointless in this feeble gravity. What good was it, in a place where everybody could do exceptional physical feats, lift extraordinary weights, jump great heights.

The MASS space station, on the other hand, had an almost perfect one gee setup. The artificial gravity produced by centrifugal spin meant there was a fractional difference experienced between the upper and lower body. This had not hampered him in any way and most people on the station never even noticed it.

But he had not been brought here as security advisor to Kane Butros, so he could spend his time training. He was here to do those things that other people couldn't, or simply wouldn't, do. *Wet work*, as he liked to call it. Although in the strange and exotic environment of Mars, there was very little *wet* involved, such was the vast range of possible ways in which a person could die up here, the opportunities for creativity were endless, and it pleased him that he was practicing his craft in a hitherto unexplored arena.

There was also the money, of course. By the time he finished his contract and returned to Earth he would be very *very* wealthy, enough to retire and live the good life, several times over. But his work was not something he wished to retire from. It was an art form, in his mind—something that just gets better with age. So he put up with the one-third gravity and began to see it as yet another opportunity to express his creativity in his craft.

He had traveled down to the surface in one of the many MASS transports and had rendezvoused with a contact in the Industrial Sector. Having studied the requirements of the assignment, he devised a plan that should deflect attention away from the true nature of the unfolding crime. His contact had already furnished him with an ID as an AsterX maintenance technician, a passcode for their mainframe and a small thumb drive.

Blake made his way to Central Logistics using his newly acquired ID to gain access to the maintenance area. He kept his head down and spoke to no one, so as to attract as little attention as possible. After a while he made it to the maintenance airlock, donned an AsterX tech EVA suit and ventured out on to the planet's surface. He was looking for the rover used by Mia Sorelli, and found it quickly, exactly where it was supposed to be, connected to the umbilical for Central Logistics. He needed to hurry now, as he only had a short window of opportunity in which to execute this part of the mission.

Entering the empty rover via the side airlock in the docking port, Blake removed his helmet and sat down in the cockpit. After a few minutes he had successfully accessed the rover's main control system and uploaded the file contained on the thumb drive. With this phase of the setup now complete he needed to get moving so he would have a chance of accomplishing the second phase of the operation.

Seventeen minutes later Blake Derringer sat in the canteen in courier central surveying all the comings and goings. If the information he had been given was correct, then he shouldn't have long to wait. His big fear was that he might be too late and have missed his opportunity. But just when he began to harbor doubts about the validity of his intel, his mind was put at rest at the sight of Mia Sorelli entering the busy canteen. He waited and watched from an inconspicuous corner as she loaded up her tray from the food dispensers and made her way to an unoccupied table at the back of the canteen. It was time now for Blake to put his game face on. He grabbed a bar and a drink from the dispenser, walked over to where Mia was sitting, and took a place on the opposite side of the table, two seats down. He nodded to her. She nodded back.

"You new here? Haven't seen you around before." He gave his best smile.

"Yeah, just a few sols." she replied.

"You like it?"

Mia looked up at him. "It's okay. I get to see more of Mars this way."

He nodded and let a moment pass. "Terrible tragedy about that guy up at Nili Fossae."

"Yeah. These things happen, I suppose."

"It's a very harsh environment here, people forget that. It's very tough on machines. I'm just back from way station 29, and there's a guy going to be stuck there for a few sols because his rover broke down. It happens all the time, a lot more than they let on." He jerked a conspiratorial thumb in the direction of Central Logistics HQ.

Mia said nothing, just offered a slight nod.

"Poor guy, I feel sorry for him. Christian, I think his name was."

Mia's ears instantly pricked up. "Who did you say?"

"Christian Smithson, I think. Why, do you know him?"

"Yeah." Mia looked down at her food for a moment. "I thought he was heading up north."

"Well, he's not going anywhere until they fix his rover." Blake laughed and shook his head.

"So where did you say he was holed up?"

"Way station 29. It's about a hundred and fifty kilometers out of Jezero, in the Isidis Basin, and he's gonna be there for a while. Like I was saying, it's a harsh environment." He sucked down the last of his drink and stood up. "Anyway, nice talking to ya, see you around." He saluted.

"Yeah, thanks."

As Blake Derringer left the canteen, a brief smile cracked his face. *The trap is set, now let's see if she takes the bait.*

15

WAY STATION 29

"We're going to way station 29." Mia moved quickly down the connecting corridor leading from Central Logistics to her rover. Gizmo was moving along beside her.

"This is not a scheduled trip," said Gizmo.

Mia stopped abruptly. "If your... programming, or whatever it is, won't allow you to go, that's fine, you stay here. But I'm going."

"This is most irregular, Mia. We have no clearance to embark on this trip. I suggest you allow me to pass a message to Dr. Jann Malbec and she can evaluate the risk/reward inherent in this endeavor."

"You do whatever you like, I'm going. It may be my only chance to catch up with this guy."

"Perhaps if you explain the nature of the operation so I can present all the data for analysis."

Mia threw her hands up in the air. "Why am I

explaining myself to a robot?" She stopped and looked at Gizmo. "Look, you infuriating bag of spare parts, this guy did me wrong. I don't expect you to understand that, but the only reason I took this gig in the first place is so I could track him down and get my stuff back."

"I see."

"No you don't, Gizmo. You're a robot, okay. Now I'm going, with or without you."

"And how are you going to operate the rover... pray tell?"

"Stop, go, left, right. How difficult can it be?" With that Mia moved off to the airlock door of the rover. Gizmo hesitated for a moment, then followed her. Mia looked back.

"So you're coming then?"

"I am afraid you leave me no choice. My responsibility is to ensure your safety. So this prerogative overrides any others."

Mia smiled at the little droid. "Well, that's good to know. Come on then, let's get moving."

THEY GOT the rover powered up and detached from the umbilical with no problems. But she had only moved a few meters when the comms burst into life.

"This is Central Logistics, this vehicle is not scheduled for operation at this time, please state your intentions."

"Eh... we're en-route to way station 29, you should have it in your system," said Mia.

"I'm sorry, we have no such record in our inventory. I insist you return to the docking hub and await further instructions."

Mia gave Gizmo a conspiratorial glance, winked and started talking in broken sentences into the comms. "This... high priority... top command... by order of... council... serious shit."

"Sorry, you're breaking up, please repeat."

Mia switched the comms off. "Okay Gizmo, let's hit the road."

The rover moved out from the central docking hub and joined the main traffic heading out of Jezero crater in the direction of the Isidis Basin. Mia estimated the trip would take over three hours, so she sat back and considered what she was going to do once she confronted Christian. Maybe she had been mistaken, maybe he didn't take her stuff after all, maybe it was still in her accommodation pod, having fallen down the back of some unit. Or maybe she had just misplaced it herself and it would show up next time she did her laundry or some other random chore. She would look a right fool, going all that way to confront him only to realize she had judged him wrong. Doubt began to creep into her thoughts. She had spent all this time and energy finding a way to get to him. Now that it was within sight, she wondered if what she was doing was right. But then again, he probably did steal it. Even Dexter and Marina, in the canteen said he was no good, things went missing when he was around.

. . .

"THAT IS STRANGE." They were nearing their destination, but it was the first time Gizmo had spoken in well over an hour.

Mia looked across. "What is?"

"I am reading anomalies in the power distribution controller."

Mia looked at the robot.

"Fluctuations inconsistent with acceptable component tolerances," it continued.

"Can you just cut to the chase, Gizmo? Is it good or bad?"

With that Mia experienced a complete brain whiteout. An intense blinding flash seemed to emanate from inside her head. At the same instant every muscle in her body spasmed in an uncontrollable convulsion. Then she blacked out.

WHEN MIA CAME TO, the first thing to register was that it was unbelievably cold. A shiver ran through her body and she started to shake uncontrollably. She got a grip on her body, literally—folding her arms around herself and rubbing some feeling back into her torso. Her breath condensed and she could see fine ice crystals feathering across the edges of the rover windshield. Mia looked over to where Gizmo was docked in the cockpit. It was still and silent.

"Gizmo?" She reached over and touched the droid. Its metal shell was icy to the touch. "Gizmo?" The robot didn't respond.

What the hell just happened? she thought. She examined the rover dash. Everything was dead, no lights, no readouts. *No power?* Only then did she begin to realize how serious her situation was. *How long have I been out?* She couldn't tell. It was long enough for the rover to lose a considerable amount of heat, but with no power that probably didn't take very long. That also meant the oxygenator was out, and CO_2 would start to build up in the cabin. *How long have I got without power?*

"Gizmo?" She shook the little robot again, but still no response. What could she do? She had no idea how to get the rover booted up again, even if that was possible. She had no way to even broadcast a mayday. Without Gizmo her chances of survival were slim to none. *Well, this is it,* she thought. *I'm going to die chasing down some ex-boyfriend.* She laughed. *I never learn, do I?*

Maybe I should get up and move around, warm myself up a bit? But then she would be using up more oxygen. So she had a choice, of sorts. Die from hypothermia or die by asphyxiation. She laughed again.

The EVA suit? Maybe it was still working. *Worth a shot.* She got out of the seat and made her way to the back of the rover where the suit was stored. She hit the power button, it booted up, lights and readouts illuminated the dim cabin interior. *Thank God.*

Mia started putting it on, but it was difficult as her

hands were numb and her body ached. She finally clipped on the helmet, leaving the visor open and checked the stats. Power was at 56%, but oxygen was only 3%. *Shit, how is that possible?* Then she remembered the diagnostics Gizmo had run on Jay Ericksen's EVA suit. It had been tampered with, sabotaged. She had bought herself a little extra time, nothing more. She turned up the heater settings, at least she would be warm when she died.

It took only a short while for some feeling to return to her numb body, the worst of the shivering had stopped and Mia could now begin to think straight. She left her visor open, choosing to use up the remaining oxygen in the rover before switching over to her EVA suit. She moved back to the cockpit and looked out the window. All around her was a flat desolate landscape. She had no idea where she was, or how far they were from way station 29, having totally relied on Gizmo for that. She looked down at the droid. Whatever happened to the rover must have affected the robot too. Some power surge probably fried its innards. It was only then that Mia realized how much she had relied on it. She was a complete fool to even contemplate this journey without it. *If only there was a way to reboot it*, she thought. Perhaps it wasn't dead, maybe it could come back online.

Mia started to examine it, looking over its metallic body, searching for something that looked like an access panel. She really had no idea what she was looking for, though. In reality she was clutching at straws, so after a short period of investigation, she gave up. There was nothing that seemed obvious to her, she simply didn't know enough about engineering to even begin to know what to look for. So Mia resorted to the only thing she could do. She gave it a kick. It rocked a little, but there was no response.

"Gizmo. I could really use your help right now." Nothing. It was no use, it was dead. So Mia launched one last massive kick. She had gotten some force behind it and the little robot was jolted out of its docking port in the cockpit. It rocked a little then went berserk. Shaking and spinning, its arms moving in all directions. Then it stopped.

Mia fell over on her ass. A result of both the kick she had given it and the shock of the response. "Gizmo?" she ventured, not sure what to expect.

The little robot's head twitched. "Mia, I seem to be missing a significant time period."

"Gizmo, you have no idea how happy I am to hear your voice."

"Why thank you, Mia. I too am very pleased to find you still functioning."

"What the hell happened?" Mia had managed to get herself upright again.

"A massive EMP."

"What's that?"

"Electromagnetic pulse. It has destroyed the rover's control systems and rendered it inert. I am afraid the rover is no longer viable. It has no functioning power source."

"What happened to you?"

"Fortunately, I am hardened against an EMP attack. However, I was unable to physically function while still docked with the rover's systems. Once you managed to undock me I regained motor control."

"Someone deliberately set some device on the rover?"

"My initial analysis suggests it was programmatically engineered."

"I have no idea what any of that means."

"Someone hacked the rover's systems and reprogrammed it to override safety protocols and generate its own EMP."

"So what you're saying is, someone just tried to kill us."

"Precisely."

"So Dr. Malbec was right." Mia's voice was low, as if she was talking to herself.

"This would be the logical conclusion."

Mia sighed. "Can you get the rover going again?"

"No, it is beyond redemption. There is nothing I can do to reanimate it."

"Great. So where the heck are we?"

"Approximately fifteen kilometers from way station 29. It's a long walk but it is possible for you to make it."

"I don't think so. My EVA suit has also been hacked, I have less than 3% oxygen."

Jezero City

"Well in that case you will be dead approximately seven kilometers before reaching it."

"Thanks for letting me know."

"My pleasure, I am here to assist."

Mia looked at the droid for a moment. "I'll pretend I didn't hear that."

"That is your prerogative. However, there is one possibility worth considering."

"At this moment Gizmo, I'll consider anything."

"I can carry you. Across this flat terrain I can attain far greater speed than you can. That means we could reach the way station within the upper limit of your oxygen reserves."

"Carry me?"

"Yes, I can carry you considerably faster than you can perambulate across the surface. There is just one caveat. And that is, you are very likely to sustain injury from the method I am proposing."

"Define injury, Gizmo."

"Minor injuries such as extensive bruising and possibly a fracture or two. Also, there is an added risk of damage to your EVA suit."

Mia looked at the droid for a moment. "Let me think. I can either sustain some injuries or die. Hmmm…. tricky one, Gizmo."

"I would opt for not dying. It would seem the better option."

"I'm joking, Gizmo." She took a look out through the

rover windscreen at the dry dusty expanse. "Okay, let's get going."

OUT ON THE surface Gizmo cradled Mia in both its arms. Mia also had a good grip around the robot's head. Once it was satisfied with the arrangement it took off at high speed. Mia had no time to think about it as the vibrations buffeted her. Even cocooned inside a tough EVA suit she could feel it. Gizmo wasn't joking. Mia felt every rock and rut as the robot ploughed on. She felt the pain mount as its speed increased. Eventually, it was all she could do to hold on.

The journey seemed eternal to Mia. She gritted her teeth and tried to ignore the intense vibrations jarring every part of her body. Then her suit started flashing a low oxygen alert. But there was nothing she could do about it. She would either make it or not. Her fate was now literally in Gizmo's hands. She felt like urging it to go faster and to hell with the pain. But she knew it was pushing itself to the limits of its ability, just to give her this one chance of staying alive. She felt herself getting weaker, she was losing her grip on the robot, and on consciousness. Finally, just when her suit was screeching its alerts the loudest, she blacked out and slipped into darkness.

16

COUNCIL SESSION

Only on very rare occasions was an extraordinary council session called. This was partly because it took time to assemble the required minimum of members, and partly because decisions made with such a diminished number could be open to appeal. The other reason, of course, was that most of the time they were simply not needed. They were, by their nature, extraordinary, and so were only required when something unprecedented happened. This was definitely one of those occasions.

The session had been in progress for a while as the formalities of calling for such a meeting were dealt with. Councilor Yuto Yamashita stood and presented the facts of the matter, as they were known to him, pertaining to the incident at Central Logistics. These facts boiled down to a courier by the name of Mia Sorelli, effectively stealing an unserviced colony rover and embarking on a reckless and wholly unauthorized journey in pursuit of her ex-boyfriend. This, by any stretch of the imagination, was a criminal act. But while this incident, heinous though it was, would not necessitate the gathering of an extraordinary council meeting, new facts had come to light that made it of major concern to the Council of Mars.

Councilor Yamashita paused in his presentation to gain the attention of the assembled members. After they were all quiet and focused on him, he continued.

"It transpires that this colonist, Ms. Mia Sorelli, only arrived on the planet six months ago. So how, you may ask, did such an inexperienced colonist get to be a courier? Not only that but it transpires that she didn't even have any training. How is this possible?" He let the question hang in the air for a brief moment. "Well, it seems that our very own Dr. Jann Malbec has abused her position as a prominent statesperson of the colony to get this rookie a position as a courier."

The assembled members looked from one to the other, reacting with gasps and murmurings of incredulity. Finally all eyes settled on Dr. Jann Malbec.

Councilor Yamashita continued. "All procedures were bypassed, all safety and training programs were simply... cast aside." he waved his sheaf of notes to emphasize this point.

Jann knew what was coming down the track at her.

"But, if that wasn't bad enough, she also chose to have that... semi-sentient droid of hers disguise itself as a G2

Jezero City

unit, threatening the safety of the wider colony population." There was an audible intake of breath at this revelation.

Jann realized that Mia, by virtue of her irresponsible actions, had just dumped her in the shit.

The Chair banged hard with his gavel as the assembly descended into chaos. "Order, order. For heaven's sake, can everyone please settle down? We'll get nowhere like this."

It took a few more attempts before some semblance of calm was restored. Then the Chair turned to Jann. "So, what do you say to these accusations, Dr. Malbec?"

What could she say? Plead innocence, when it was patently all true? So, she chose instead to go on the attack. "I have watched from the sidelines for too long as this colony that we fought so hard to create, has grown fat and complacent on its own success. But let's not forget how this *success* was won—by knowing who our enemies were and meeting them head on."

Councilor Yamashita scoffed. "I can't see how this has any relevance to the issue being discussed. This is just the usual paranoid bullshit we have grown to expect from Dr. Malbec."

The Chair rapped his gavel. "Councilor Yamashita, I insist that you show some respect here in the council chamber, and desist from personal rebukes." He then turned to Jann. "Dr. Malbec, please continue."

"Thank you." Jann nodded to the Chair. "You all know my opinions here, and yes some may say I am... overly suspicious. But it has served me well in the past. But for it, I wouldn't be here—and neither would any of you, for that matter."

"Be that as it may, the past is the past. We have moved on," said Yuto.

"Yes, get to the point, Dr. Malbec," urged the Chair.

"The point is, I do not believe that the incident over at Nili Fossae was an accident. I think he was killed deliberately to hide something—something that could threaten all of us."

"This is nonsense. We've been over all this before. I think Dr. Malbec has finally lost her marbles." Councilor Yuto Yamashita appealed to the Chair.

The Chair rapped his gavel again. "With all due respect, Dr. Malbec, this is old ground. Your feelings on this matter have been discussed several times and, without exception, have been shown to be unfounded. I think you need to return to the matter at hand. Which is why you saw fit to abuse your position and set up a very inexperienced colonist as a courier?"

"Because I'm not going to sit here and watch everything I have fought for be destroyed by the naiveté of this council. That courier was murdered, and since none of you were going to do anything about it, I decided to investigate. Mia Sorelli, far from being inexperienced, was a highly regarded homicide detective back on Earth. So in my opinion, she is the single best individual on the planet to find out what the hell is going on!"

The council chamber again descended into chaos,

and the Chair almost broke his gavel trying to regain order. When some semblance of discipline had been established he returned his attention to Jann. "If I may speak for the council as a whole, we have nothing but the greatest respect for what you have done in the past to help build the colony into what it is today." He looked around at the assembled councilors. There was a tacit agreement, acknowledged by nodding and murmuring.

"But it seems you misjudged this... Ms. Sorelli, since she went off on her own wild goose chase, in pursuit of an ex-lover, of all things. This is not the modus operandi of a professional, wouldn't you agree?"

"She was tricked into that. In my mind it adds further evidence that someone is playing us for fools."

"The only fool around here is you Dr. Malbec." This interjection by Yamashita allowed a flood of similar opinions to take over the proceedings for a few moments before the Chair could wrest back control.

"Whatever your views on the incident, you simply cannot take the law into your own hands anymore, this is not the Wild West. Your personal paranoia over vague and shadowy plots has led to this unfortunate event. Furthermore, you have put the entire colony in danger, not simply by allowing this colonist to do whatever the hell she likes, but by allowing that robot of yours to go roaming around on its own."

"I don't know why we allow that robot to exist in the first place. It's just too dangerous. I say the time has come to dismantle it once and for all." Councilor Yamashita was on his feet again.

Jann jumped up from her seat and leaned across the table. "That robot has played a significant role in the formation of this colony. It has saved my ass more than once so I owe it, in fact you *all* do. It is my friend and anyone who puts a finger on it to dismantle it will need to get through me first."

"It's a potentially dangerous machine, and the only reason it has been allowed to exist is because you and Nills Langthorp have such an attachment to it. You are supposed to keep it on a short leash, not let it wander off where it likes. You are putting us in a difficult position, Dr. Malbec." The Chair sighed and sat back.

"I think this might be a good time to take a break and let passions on both sides cool down. When we resume we will have to decide on what disciplinary action to take. That is all. We will resume in one hour." The Chair tapped his gavel again and Jann stood up and walked out of the council chamber—alone.

It was at that moment she realized how far from the levels of power she had fallen. With Nills too far away to make the session, she didn't have a single friend on the council. They were all against her. What sympathies she mustered in some were evaporating fast. They were seeing her as a lame duck and running the other way. She was alone, she had to face the truth—the council were never going to listen to her. She had failed.

. . .

Jezero City

JANN REMOVED herself to one of the contemplative areas within the garden surrounding the council dais, far enough away that it didn't interfere with her thoughts. This particular spot was her favorite, flanked on all sides by tall trees and trailing vines. In the center was a low fountain, and around it were several stone seats, hewn from solid blocks of Martian granite transported all the way from Elysium. She sat down and receded into her thoughts.

It was not long before her reverie was interrupted by a tall figure entering her space. It was Evon Dent, operations director of the Mars Alliance Scientific Survey.

"My apologies, Dr. Malbec. I do not wish to intrude, but would it be possible to have a moment of your time?"

Jann eyed him with suspicion. *What the hell does he want?* She nodded to the stone bench opposite her. "Take a seat."

He sat down and looked around. Jann figured it was not because he wanted to take in the scenery, but more to check that they were alone and unobserved. "For what it's worth, Dr. Malbec, I'm beginning to think there might be some validity in your... suspicions."

Jann's ears pricked up. Had she heard him right? She didn't reply, just looked at him intently.

"I appreciate that we have not seen eye-to-eye on certain issues, and that.... well, there are those who view the work we do here as... overly clandestine. But..." and he looked around again before leaning in and lowering his voice. "I think that you may be right about the accident up at Nili Fossae... not being an accident, as such."

"As such?" Jann was intrigued now.

Evon shifted in his seat. Jann was getting the sense that this was not easy for him to admit, considering all that had just transpired.

"There is a general perception, I think, that MASS is one big homogeneous agency, dedicated to the advancement of scientific knowledge of Mars." He paused. "I wish that were the case. But it's not so. Not unlike the politics here in the colony, we too have our factions. Some who would choose to go beyond our remit." He raised his hands, palms out. "I know, I know, this is also many other people's perception of us, but I assure you it is not what we are about."

"I appreciate your candor, Evon, but so what? We all know this. Anyway, you know more about the accident than anyone as you've been sitting on the evidence, doing exactly nothing."

"That's the thing. We don't know, because every time I inquire as to the progress of the investigation, I get the feeling I'm being stonewalled."

"Meaning?"

"Meaning, that I think, like you, that someone or some group within MASS doesn't want the results out in the open. In short, Dr. Malbec, I think someone is leading us on a merry dance."

Evon did another of his quick scans of their

surroundings starting in again. "It may come as a surprise to you, but we have a gap in our records concerning Jay Eriksen. It seems that he disappeared from our official database for the best part of four sols. But if someone were to locate the rover's recorder, we would know where it was during that time, and possibly get some idea as to what Jay Eriksen might have been up to."

Jann considered this revelation for a moment. "So how can we do that?"

"I was hoping you might be able to help in that regard."

Jann considered this request. "Here's the thing, Evon. I don't know which is more disconcerting. The fact that I may be right in my suspicions, or the fact that you seem to have lost so much trust in your own organization that you want *my* help."

"Anyway, I don't see how I can help. As you can tell from the reception I just got in the council meeting, I'm fast running out of options. Unless, that is, my errant agent decides to stop screwing around and come back on radar."

17

REBOOT

A brilliant fluorescent light burned its way through to Mia's retina and into her optic nerve. She shut her eyelids tight and instinctively moved a hand to cover her face. A sharp pain shot up her arm, making her cry out.

"Mia, you have returned to the land of the living." It was Gizmo. "For a moment there, I thought you might be past saving. But I see you are made of superior biomass than the average Earthling."

"Where... am... I?" Mia's throat felt like she had just eaten a cheese grater.

"At way station 29. We made it here just in time."

Mia sat up, very slowly. More stabbing pain punctuated her movements. Her chest burned. She looked down to find her flight suit had been ripped open.

"CPR," said Gizmo. It pointed to a defibrillator beside

the bed. "I needed to reboot you. It took a few attempts before you restarted."

Mia clutched her chest. Her skin was raw and she felt like someone had driven a herd of cattle over her. "Thanks," was the best she could manage. Mia could see they were in the small medbay. "Anyone else here?"

"No, just us."

"How long have I been out?"

"Not long, approximately seven minutes."

Mia moved into a standing position, one hand still holding the edge of the bed. "Oh my god, my entire body is seriously banged up. I don't think there's anywhere that I don't have pain." She moved over to the small workspace and started to open drawers. "Painkillers, I need lots of painkillers."

It took Mia five minutes of searching and label reading before she could finally sit down in the main common area and take stock of her situation. The droid had not used the comms to send any distress message yet, even though they were now technically stranded. The rover was damaged beyond Gizmo's ability to repair, so the only way back to civilization was to call for help. But that could alert whoever was trying to kill her that she was still alive.

"Do you have a way of contacting Dr. Malbec that can't be traced?"

"I can send an encrypted message, but I will need to relay it through the way station comms antennae, as I do not possess sufficient range."

"Can that be traced?"

"While the contents would be indecipherable, the transmission would indeed be noted."

Mia thought about this. Her only other option was to wait and hitch a ride on the next courier through here, but it could be several sols before anyone else showed up. And with the migration of all citizens to Jezero City for the celebrations, she would be stranded here until after that.

"Gizmo, get a message to Jann. Tell her someone just tried to kill me and that we're stranded out here."

"Will do." It buzzed off to the comms desk.

Mia relaxed a bit as the effects of the painkillers began to kick in. She knew there wasn't much one could do for cracked ribs but she decided to bandage herself up, just to give her torso some support. Her left wrist was also swollen and extremely painful to move, so it too would need wrapping.

As she tended to her injuries she considered why someone wanted her dead. It wasn't because she knew too much. So far, she knew absolutely nothing other than hints. But whoever was after her knew that she was on the hunt, investigating, seeking out the truth. And it must be, that if she kept at it, then the truth would out eventually—whatever the hell it was. So she must be closer than she realized. But where would she find it? Where to next? Had Jay Eriksen also been searching? Did he find something that had got him killed?

"Mia!" Gizmo came whizzing into the medbay. "I have

picked up a rover, approximately five klicks east of us, heading this way."

Mia looked surprised. "That was quick."

"It is a MASS rover. Should I try to contact it?"

"No, wait, let's think this through first. Is it coming from where we abandoned the rover?"

"Yes."

"Well, it's way too soon for Dr. Malbec to have mounted a rescue. So I think we need to consider that this situation is not good. It could be that whoever is out to kill me was following us, making sure the job was done. So now that they've found our rover empty, they're going to the only place we could be, here in this way station."

Mia realized she was effectively trapped, with no escape. She had no weapons, and in her current weakened state she would not be able to defend herself from a direct assault. What's more, there could be several people in the approaching rover, all hell bent on her destruction. *Think*, she said to herself.

It was also entirely possible that this was a genuine mission. Then Mia would be in a very awkward position, waiting for them to show themselves to be a threat. And when that happened, it would be too late.

"Gizmo, can you disable comms here? Not permanently, but for a few hours?"

"Yes, I think I can rig something to do that, a simple battery relay switch on the main antennae should do it. Once the battery drained it would flip back on."

"Okay, let's get to it. Follow me and I'll explain the plan."

GIZMO HAD ESTIMATED around ten minutes before the rover arrived, so Mia didn't have much time. They moved out of the common area and into a short tunnel with airlocks spaced out on either side. This was where the visiting rovers could connect, but they could also be used as standard airlocks for venturing outside on to the surface. Mia quickly got into a spare EVA suit. Each way station had at least two of these, fully resourced. She booted it up and checked the heads-up display for alerts. When she was sure everything was okay, she took a deep breath, flipped her visor down, and entered the airlock.

As she waited for the volume to equalize with the outside atmosphere, she wondered if she was doing the right thing. She had assumed that whoever was driving the rover would head straight for the nearest airlock and dock. But if they were being cautious, they might drive around the way station first, check it out to make sure there were no surprises waiting. If that was the case then she would be spotted—there was no place to hide out here, no place to run.

The outer door opened and Gizmo wasted no time in speeding off across the surface to the antennae, to temporarily disable it. Then it would make its way back inside the way station while Mia waited outside. It would tuck itself into a corner of the docking tunnel, out of the way, and power itself down to make it look like it was in sleep mode. To the untrained eye it would look like any other G2 unit—parked out of the way, waiting to be assigned some tasks, or simply just non-functioning, waiting for repair. Either way, Mia was hoping it would go unnoticed. Then again, she was hoping for a lot of elements to go her way if this crazy plan of hers was going to work.

Fortunately the base of the antennae array could not be seen from the direction the rover was approaching. But Gizmo still had to finish the hack and then make it back inside before the MASS rover docked. Mia resisted the temptation to move out and around the side of the docking tunnel to see how close it was, just in case she was seen. It frustrated her because she couldn't hear it coming either, all she heard, inside the EVA suit, was the sound of her own breathing.

The droid was taking an eternity. *What the hell is keeping it?* She slowed her breathing and tried to calm down, and reminded herself that Gizmo was smart beyond belief, so it had probably calculated all the possible parameters, trajectories and vectors. Mia tried hard to convince herself that the robot had it all worked out to the last picosecond.

She was beginning to tire. Her body was still weak from her near-fatal dash across the surface. She sat down, resting her back against the outer skin of the docking tunnel, and forced herself to slow her heart rate. That was when she felt a subtle vibration. Standing up again and placing both hands on the docking tunnel wall, she could feel the vibration in the building. The rover was very close now. Then there was a thump. *Shit, it's docked.* She turned around to see where Gizmo was, and saw it disappear into the airlock—the little droid was cutting it very tight.

On the one hand Mia breathed a sigh of relief that whoever was driving the MASS rover had not decided to do a quick scout of the area, but on the other hand she wondered if Gizmo had left itself with enough time. It needed to be in position before the airlock opened and disgorged its occupants into the way station.

She could feel the thump and whirr of the airlock motors as they ran through their sequences by keeping her hands pressed against the docking tunnel skin. Finally, after a few fretful moments, it went quiet. She stepped back. *Has Gizmo done it?* Mia turned and walked to the very end of the docking tunnel, turned the corner, and very tentatively peered around to see the nose of the rover. She waited.

She could see it rock slightly as something heavy moved inside it, then Gizmo appeared at the controls. The little robot had done it. The rover started up, detached itself from the dock and moved out towards Mia. She came out of her hiding place and waved to Gizmo. It responded by giving a kind of thumbs up gesture.

Mia ran to the rear airlock as the rover came past. The outer door was already open and she clambered inside.

As soon as the door closed she felt the rover pick up speed, away from way station 29. She exited the airlock, removed her helmet and gloves, and sat in the cockpit seat beside Gizmo.

"Well done." She slapped the robot on the back and instantly regretted it, as pain shot up her arm.

"Thank you, but it was elementary. And, if I may say, it was an excellent plan, Mia."

"I don't believe it, am I getting a compliment?"

"Credit where credit is due, is that not the common saying in these circumstances?"

Mia rubbed the pain out of her wrist as she slumped back into the co-pilot seat. "So how many were there?"

"Just one, see here." Gizmo played a video feed on the rover's main screen. It was shaky at first then steadied to show a view down the length of the docking tunnel. From the right hand side a figure entered, tall, hard to tell what age. He held a small plasma weapon. He stopped, looking up and down the tunnel before resting his eyes on Gizmo. Mia recognized him. It was the guy from the canteen, the one who set her up. On screen, he had moved in closer to inspect the G2 unit, then turned back to go down the tunnel and into the way station. The video went shaky again as Gizmo made for the airlock.

So who the hell is he? Mia wondered. "Gizmo, can you interrogate the rover's log and see where it's been?"

The video was replaced by a long scrolling list. Mia moved the screen closer to her and began to tap on some of the entries to bring up more detail. The rover departed from MASS HQ around the same time as she and Gizmo had absconded from courier central, and it had taken the same route. It had been following them.

Mia moved the screen out of the way. "Well, that just confirms what we already know."

She glanced around the rover. Even though it was a MASS vehicle it was exactly the same as all the others. They were all made here on Mars, in the factories in the Industrial Sector, as a joint venture between the colony and AsterX. There was nothing to distinguish this one from any of the others. Except for one thing.

"Gizmo, if this rover left from MASS HQ then their systems will have no problem accepting it back at the main dock."

"That is correct. It is tagged for their systems, so it has access to all MASS installations."

"Okay, then. Let's head for MASS HQ."

"Very well. What is your plan?"

"How long before the comms come back on at the way station?"

"I calculate three hours and thirty-nine minutes."

"And how long before we get to MASS HQ?"

"Approximately three hours."

"That should be enough for us to get in there and do a bit of snooping."

"What are we looking for?"

"Assuming Jay Eriksen was killed to keep him quiet, either he knew too much or stumbled upon something he shouldn't have, then knowing where he had been in the time leading up to his death would give us some clues as to what's going on. One thing's for sure, MASS are involved in it somehow."

THEY DROVE in silence for what seemed like an eternity to Mia. Eventually she saw the landscape changing as the rim of Jezero Crater began to grow on the horizon.

"We will shortly be within range to make direct comms contact with Dr. Malbec," said Gizmo.

A few minutes later an encrypted inbound comms connection flickered onto the monitor, and Dr. Jann Malbec's head and shoulders materialized on screen.

"Mia, what the hell are you doing? Chasing down your ex-boyfriend is not part of the plan." Her voice was surprisingly calm and measured.

"I know, I'm sorry about that, but I was set up. Those bastards knew how to get to me, how to get me somewhere they could get rid of me. They sabotaged the rover and except for Gizmo they would have succeeded in doing the same thing to me as they did to Jay Eriksen."

"Yeah, I told you Gizmo's a useful friend to have in a jam. So where are you now?" said Jann.

"Long story short, we stole a rover from the guy who's trying kill me. He's stuck at way station 29. We're heading back to Jezero."

"Look Mia, your crazy stunt has hit the headlines here. I've just been hauled over the coals for it. What's more, your cover is blown, and the council are out to find you and Gizmo. You've been deemed a threat to the colony."

"That's bullshit. Can't they see what's going on?"

"No, they can't, or won't—that's the problem. It's been the problem all along, that's why I wanted someone like you to investigate."

Mia rubbed her forehead. "I'm sorry, Jann. I'll be straight with you, I took this job so I could track down my ex and get my stuff back. I didn't really believe you about the Eriksen guy. I thought you were just being... well, paranoid."

"Welcome to the club, everybody else seems to have the same opinion of me."

"Well not anymore, surely they must see there's a major threat imminent?"

"Mia, you must understand my power to influence is fast being eroded, and your stunt didn't help that. Each time I make the case I look more and more deranged in their eyes. As it stands at the moment, all citizens are being called back to Jezero City for the celebrations later today, so everyone's energy has been focused on that. I'm fast running out of options here."

There was a silence as Mia contemplated just how much she had screwed up. "Look, someone just tried to kill me. The fundamental question is why? What do they not want us to find out? Whatever it is, it's got to do with Jay Eriksen, so we're going back to the MASS HQ to take a closer look at that rover. Gizmo also thinks he can hack their database and find out where Jay was in the sols before the accident."

"You won't find anything in the database," said Jann.

Mia was a little taken aback by this response. "How do you know that?"

"It seems my entreaties to the council have not completely fallen on deaf ears. I have managed to gain one, quite surprising, ally. None other than Evon Dent, the MASS operations director. It would appear he has suspicions similar to mine."

Mia think about this. "The MASS director?" was all that she could muster as a reply.

"His own investigations are being blocked. By whom and for what reason, he doesn't know. But he has managed to ascertain there are several sols missing from Jay Eriksen's records."

"Well if he's mister big over at MASS why doesn't he just stroll right on in and demand answers?"

"You don't understand that people like myself and Evon are like great big container ships at sea. Everybody can see us coming for miles and it takes us forever to maneuver, we're anything but agile and stealthy. Him walking in and knocking heads would do nothing but alert the threat and drive it completely underground."

"There must be something we can do. Are these rovers tracked in any way, I mean do they have a black box or something like on an airplane?"

"You're correct, they do. And that is exactly what Evon

suggested looking for. But we don't know where it is, or how to get it."

"Well, most likely it's still with the remains of the rover in MASS HQ, and fortunately we happen to be driving in a stolen MASS rover. Maybe I can find a way to sneak in again." Mia paused for a moment as a plan was beginning to form in her mind. "Jann, all citizens are being called back to Jezero City, what about the MASS guys, and the contractors?"

"Those who can will also come over here for the celebrations. Others are going up to their space station to watch the terraforming event from orbit."

"Can you get Evon Dent to issue a directive to clear everyone out of HQ?"

"Yes, I think that's possible. I mean it's going to happen later today anyway."

"Good, do that. Gizmo and I will find a way in and get that black box. Then, maybe we can get some answers."

18

DROID DOWN

Mia had taken over driving the rover. She reckoned she had to learn sometime, but in reality it was simply to break the boredom of the return journey. She still had her EVA suit on but had removed the helmet and gloves. She couldn't wait to get out of it, but for the moment she thought it prudent to keep herself wrapped up in it—just in case.

As they approached the Industrial Sector, she was happy to see that the normal sol-to-sol traffic was greatly diminished. Citizens had been making their way to Jezero City for the celebrations, and the population of the outlying facilities had thinned out. Those that were not citizens, the contractors and tourists, were not obliged to be at the main city, but most who could had elected to head over and join in the festivities. Of course some of those lucky enough to work for the Mars Alliance Scientific Survey could disembark from the planet up to their orbiting space station where they could watch the event unfold in real time. As Mia and Gizmo moved further into the crater, she could see the liftoff of one of these transports. Hopefully Jann had managed to get most of the staff at the MASS HQ cleared out by now. All this movement of people left the crater feeling oddly empty. This suited Mia, as she was less likely to be stopped and boarded by the Colony authorities that wanted to find her and the rogue robot, Gizmo.

As they approached the leading edge of the Industrial Sector, Mia turned right off the main road and headed for the MASS facility. She could see its domed roof rising up as they got closer. The long curving rover dock was completely devoid of vehicles. *The place must be deserted,* she thought. *Good.*

"Gizmo, can you take the controls and bring us in?"

"Certainly. Anywhere in particular?"

"I don't suppose it matters."

GIZMO REVERSED the rover up to the first available bay and docked. Then followed the usual humming of motors and clunking of gears as the rover connected up to the main facility. There was a momentary flicker as power was transferred from the rover to the central systems.

Mia hesitated for a fraction of a second as she considered getting out of the bulky EVA suit before entering the facility. But leaving it on had its advantages, even without the helmet and gloves. It offered some protection from attack, although it made her less agile. On balance, she decided to leave it on.

The rear rover airlock opened up to an empty space, much to Mia's relief. It seemed everyone had taken up the opportunity to clock off early and enjoy the festivities. So far so good. They slowly made their way through the facility to where the remains of Jay Eriksen's rover were located. As far as Mia could tell nothing had changed. Everything was pretty much as she and Gizmo had last seen it. They split up and started searching.

Like a black box in an airplane, it was not in fact black, but bright yellow, so in theory it should be easy to spot. But after a few minutes of searching, both the interior of the rover shell and all the components arrayed on the workbenches, they couldn't find it. This came as no surprise to Mia. She had pretty much regarded this plan as only a few notches above futile, considering the first thing anyone would do would be to hide the evidence of the rover's journey history.

Mia turned around when she heard the door to the maintenance area open. The facility was not completely empty, there was someone else here. Her first thought was to hide, but she was too late. Standing right in front of her was the same guy she had met in the airlock entrance on her first sortie to the MASS HQ. She stood still for a moment deciding what to do, then she waved and said, "Hi."

He did a double take and Mia could almost see the

wheels in his brain turning, trying to figure out what to do, or say.

"How come you're not over at Jezero City enjoying the party?" she ventured.

"Eh... someone's got to stay here," he managed hesitantly by way of reply.

"Say, you didn't happen to see a bright yellow box about so big lying around here somewhere?" Mia did a box shape with her hands.

"Eh... well, yeah. There's one in the control room over there. It's kinda hard to miss."

"Gee, thanks. I'll make sure to mention you to Evon Dent when I meet him later. You've been a great help." Mia started off toward the control room. *Well that was easy,* she thought.

"Wait a minute, who are you anyway? There's not supposed to be any people in here."

Then again maybe not. She turned back and walked toward him.

"Look, you're a nice guy, but I'm in a bit of a hurry, so please don't take this personally." She punched him square in the face. He dropped.

"Gizmo?"

The little robot whizzed in beside her and scanned the prostrate form on the floor. "I see you have been busy."

"Find me some zip-ties or something to tie this guy up with."

. . .

Soon, the hapless MASS employee had been trussed up and parked against a wall. Mia and Gizmo were in the control room where the little droid was interfacing the black box with one of the room's terminals. Mia watched on the main screen as Gizmo set to work interrogating its database. Lines of code scrolled down the monitor, interspersed with a multitude of windows opening and closing in rapid succession.

"Access granted," said Gizmo as the screen displayed an itemized list of Jay Eriksen's itinerary during his short employ with MASS. And it was short. Mia counted no more than seven lines. Starting four sols before his fatal journey up to Nili Fossae.

His first sol started from the AsterX maintenance yards, where he picked up a recently serviced rover. From there he made his way to a MASS research station at the very edge of Jezero. Mia tapped an icon to get more information on this. It was marked simply as *Biotech*. He stopped for less than an hour before heading out of Jezero and north to another MASS facility. This was labeled 'TNCP.'

"Gizmo, have you any idea what that is? Mia pointed to the cryptic acronym.

"Thermo-nuclear central processing."

Mia raised an eyebrow at the droid. She went back to following the trail.

Jay Eriksen spent a night in this facility before making the return journey all the way back to Jezero City, where he spent two sols parked at one of the rover docks on the outskirts. *What was he doing there for that long?* After that, he journeyed to MASS HQ for a one hour stop before embarking on his final, fatal trip up to Nili Fossae. The itinerary ended there. Mia sat back and scratched her head; she really needed a shower.

"Does this have an audio recording? I mean does it record the conversations in the cockpit?"

"Yes, it records as much data as possible."

"Can you go back to when he arrived at the TNCP, and then to when he was leaving it?"

Mia listened as scratchy audio of the dead man's conversations echoed around the control room. Mostly it was just mundane data, but one phrase caught her attention. It was the same time as he was undocking from the TNCP. Some controller was speaking to him. *...and remember, Jay, this needs to be in position, and all set up before the terraforming event, otherwise it will all be for nothing.*

Mia sat in silence for a moment as the wheels of her own brain began to work. Finally she turned to Gizmo. "What goes on in TNCP?"

"It coordinates all nuclear activity on the planet. Including monitoring, storage and reprocessing."

"Would that include the terraforming event?"

"Not the event itself. But they would have oversight of all the nuclear devices."

Mia began to think the unthinkable. "How big are these devices, Gizmo? I mean, could one fit in a rover?"

"Quite easily, they are not very big. Easily managed by one person or a G2 unit."

"Oh shit." Mia stood up. "I don't believe it."

"What?"

Mia shook her head. "Tell me if you think this is rational, Gizmo. I think Jay Eriksen has hidden a nuclear device somewhere in Jezero City, and it's linked to the terraforming event later this sol."

"That is indeed consistent with the data."

"Oh my god. Quick, you need to get this information to Dr. Malbec now. And tell her… she has got to stop that detonation from taking place… somehow."

Gizmo was silent for a moment. "Done."

"Okay, let's get the hell out of here."

THEY MADE their way back to the rover without incident. Mia considered it was probably time to head back to Jezero City, even though the council were actively looking for them. But with the new evidence that Mia had uncovered, that would change and more resources would be brought to bear. But time was running out. The terraforming event was going to take place in less than seven hours. Mia wasted no time in getting herself strapped in to the cockpit as Gizmo took the controls. But when Mia glanced out the window she could see another vehicle had docked while they were inside the HQ.

"Gizmo, looks like we've got company." She pointed.

"Let's get going." But the rover didn't move. "What's wrong?"

"Manual control has been overridden by the central systems."

"Can you hack it?"

"Working on it."

Mia waited getting an uneasy feeling. Then a horrendous grinding noise emanated from the outside of the rear airlock.

"Gizmo, hurry... I think someone is trying to get the airlock door open."

The rover burst into life and lurched forward, disconnecting from the dock.

"Come on, let's get out of here." Mia flipped on the rear view monitor, and watched the MASS HQ building recede into the background. "Who the hell was that?"

"I think the individual we left at way station 29 might have found a way to communicate with MASS HQ, or even found a way back here."

"Goddammit." Mia hung on to her seat as the rover sped across the open terrain. They were heading past the AsterX maintenance yards at the very edge of the Industrial Sector, around half a kilometer away. The ground suddenly got a lot rougher as Gizmo had taken them off-road.

She was beginning to breathe a little easier when something big hit the rover and Mia saw the world spinning through the front window. The rover tumbled over and over before coming to a rocky halt, right way up.

"What the..." She found herself lying flat on her back in the center aisle. Alerts were flashing all across the dash.

"Decompression!" Gizmo blared. "Get your helmet on."

She looked around. *Where the hell is it?* Both her helmet and gloves had been flung around the interior of the vehicle when it cartwheeled. She spotted it lying against the rear airlock and crawled back to grab it. She could feel the skin on her face stinging and her breathing was labored. She took a deep breath and held it, then she wondered if that was the right procedure during decompression. Would her lungs explode? *Screw it.* She grabbed the helmet and snapped it on, along with the one glove that was still inside it. *Where's the other one?* Her EVA suit wouldn't boot up without it.

The rover jolted forward and stopped again. Gizmo must be trying to restart it. *Shit, shit, where's that glove?* She found it wedged behind a storage container, grabbed it and clipped it on. Her suit came to life and immediately registered the decompression and flipped her visor closed. Mia exhaled and took a tentative breath as she looked up to where Gizmo was still trying to get the rover moving again. The little droid's head flipped around as the emergency hatch blew out. Mia was thrown forward as the last of the cabin's air evacuated.

Through the gap she could see a suited figure raise a handheld weapon and fire at Gizmo. The little droid was encased in a bright flashing cage of electrical craziness. It sparked and shook as its circuits were battered by the plasma blast.

Gizmo, no! Mia shouted inside her suit. She went back down the center of the cabin, away from the source of the blast. Going forward was not an option, her only chance now was to get out and on open ground. She didn't want to be trapped inside. She opened the rear airlock and Gizmo was hit by another blast from the plasma gun.

A few seconds later Mia fell out onto the dusty Martian surface and scrambled to get to her feet. On her left she could see the rover that crashed into them, it was only a few meters away and looked to have suffered only minor damage. She made a dash for it, and had just set one foot inside its airlock when she felt a thump on her left shoulder. Her suit screamed alerts and its systems went into shutdown. *Goddammit.* She closed the outer door and hit the compression button, just as her suit died. She must have taken a direct hit, but the energy from the plasma burst dissipated through the suit rather than through her. Mia charged into the cockpit and began to reverse the rover as fast as possible. She could still see the figure out on the surface running after her. He raised his weapon and fired again. A bright flashing energy ball burst across the windshield, but it held. Mia spun the rover around and gave it maximum throttle as she sped off towards the AsterX maintenance yards.

By the time Mia drove up to the main entrance doors her left shoulder had gone numb and all down her side she had a tingling sensation. She must have taken more damage than she realized from the plasma weapon. She was not that familiar with how they worked, all her training had been in ballistic weapons. But they were extremely dangerous in the pressurized confines of space. You were more likely to kill yourself rupturing whatever containment was keeping you alive, than inflicting any damage on your target. Pulsed energy plasma (PEP) was a lot more useful. It used a high-energy blast, and had the advantage of being non-lethal if necessary. Mia doubted that her assailant had set his to stun. The only reason she was still standing was because of the rugged EVA suit.

Another advantage of PEP weapons was that they could fry any electronics that happened to be in the way of the blast. So Mia reckoned that Gizmo was probably a goner. There was just no way it could have survived several direct hits. She felt its loss. *Poor Gizmo*, she thought. She had grown used to its quirky ways, even grown to like it. But now it was gone, she was on her own, and being hunted down—it would only be a matter of time before the attacker caught up with her. She had only a few minutes head start.

As the entrance doors to the maintenance yard came into view, Mia considered that there was nothing stopping her from driving somewhere else, back to Jezero City maybe. Why was she coming here?

The rover died. *What? No, not now.* Mia thumped the dashboard in frustration. It flicked on and off a few times then came back online. Her decision was made. She pushed the throttle and headed for the yard entrance.

Her EVA suit was shot and this rover was on the way out so she really had no other option. The massive entrance doors opened automatically as she approached. The volume of space inside the airlock could accommodate at least a half dozen rovers and then some. Mia drove in and the outer door began to close. It took a few more minutes before it could be pressurized, then the inner door opened to reveal a huge area full of machines of every conceivable shape and size, most in various states of disassembly. Mia got out and started threading her way through the maze.

"Hello?" she shouted, her voice echoing off the high domed ceiling. "Anyone there?" There was no answer. As she expected, all workers had decamped to Jezero City for the celebrations. Mia was on her own. She froze. She thought she had heard something, movement maybe. She listened intently—there it was, a hum. The sound of the airlock doors opening again. She ran.

Mia was finding it hard to move fast as her left side was dull and numb, as if she had been sitting on her leg for a while and it was having trouble getting blood recirculating. She hopped more than ran. *This is no good.* She could not outrun the threat. The only other options were to hide, or to make a stand. There were plenty of places to hide, but Mia knew that it would just be a matter of time before he found her. She was a wounded animal being hunted down. The only option was to fight back.

Mia looked around, trying to find something to use as

a weapon. There were lots of heavy tools, good for bludgeoning. But in her weakened state how much force could she bring to the battle? Something sharp would be better. A spear, maybe. That was Malbec's weapon of choice; she had developed a lot of skill with it. Legend had it she could skewer a victim through the eye at fifty paces. But Mia did not have much time to think about the merits of various weapons. Whatever she could find quickly would have to do.

In the end it came down to a long thin flat-headed screwdriver. It had a stem at least twenty centimeters long, presumably for getting to screws in very inaccessible locations. Mia was going to press it into service as a stiletto. She also grabbed a handful of bolts and shoved them into a pocket. Her next move was to find a good place to launch an attack. She was looking for height, a place where she would have the upper hand, where she could land on top of him and use her momentum to drive home her weapon. She clambered up the side of a parked rover, lay down flat on the roof, and waited.

In the distance she could hear the hum of the airlock doors operating again. *Was he leaving?* That didn't make any sense to her. Then she heard a shuffling sound. It was close, only a few meters away. She took some of the bolts out of her pocket and threw them on the workbench beside the rover. It had the desired effect. The shuffling stopped and she could just make out his shadow coming closer to investigate the source of the sound.

He moved with stealth, keeping his back to the rover. When Mia judged that he was directly beneath her she leaped off the roof, aiming to plunge the screwdriver into his jugular. She missed and drove it into his shoulder instead. He yelled in pain as Mia tumbled to the floor. She was flat on her back looking up at him when he raised his weapon and fired. Mia rolled as a bright blue ball of electrical death hit the floor beside her. She avoided a direct hit, but it was enough to send a high-voltage charge rippling through her lower body. She screamed as every fiber of her being was convulsed in a raging storm of energy. The pain was excruciating, as if every muscle in her body had gone into cramp all at once.

As the pain receded Mia was left a trembling mess, totally numb from the waist down. She finally raised herself up on one elbow. Her attacker was glaring down at her while he pulled the screwdriver out of his bloodied shoulder.

"You know," he said as he threw it on the ground beside her, "up until this point, I've been enjoying our little chase around Mars. It's been a while since a target has been as sporting as you have." He raised a hand to his forehead in a mock salute. "I tip my hat to you for that."

"Screw you," said Mia

"Ah... a fighter to the end. I admire that. But, I'm afraid it's time to go." He raised the gun and pointed it at Mia's head.

"Tell me why."

He regarded her intensely, then lowered his gun.

"Why?" He seemed to have to think about this for a second or two. "Well, since you've been such good hunting, I'll tell you. It's because it's my job to kill you."

"Well, it's not going to make a difference. You're too late now. They already know about the plan to destroy Jezero City with a nuke. The event will be canceled, so you lose."

"Nukes?" He threw his head back and laughed until he started to cough and clutched his chest, which was saturated with blood from the wound Mia had inflicted on him. "Is that your plan? To kill me by making me laugh?"

He raised the gun again. "You really haven't a clue, do you? It's not a nuke, it's a bioweapon, and believe me it is far from canceled. Now, if you don't mind, Miss Sorelli, it is time to die."

Mia watched helplessly as he raised his weapon. This was it and there was not a damn thing she could do about it.

But before he could fire, another plasma ball hurtled in from nowhere and hit him smack in the side. His body shook in a violent shimmering incandescence as every nerve of his being was ripped to shreds. He slumped to his knees, his eyes lifeless, and collapsed face down on the ground in front of Mia. As the last of the plasma charge fizzled out a thin filament of smoke drifted slowly up from his skull.

It took Mia a few seconds to drag her eyes away from the corpse to locate the source of the shot.

"Gizmo?" The little robot stood some distance away. From its breastplate Mia could see the muzzle of a PEP weapon. "I thought you were dead."

The robot whizzed over to where Mia lay on the ground. "Technically I was never alive to begin with."

Mia slumped back on the floor, looking straight up at the droid. "Well, I'm really happy you're still functioning. How the hell did you survive those blasts?"

"I am hardened against such electromagnetic attacks. I did sustain some temporary trauma to my systems, but since a significant percentage of my mind resides in the Jezero City mainframe I was able to reboot myself and am approximately 89.73% functional."

Mia groaned as she tried to move. "I'm all beat up, Gizmo. I don't suppose you can reboot me."

"You will find the effects of the plasma blast to be temporary. Assuming you have not sustained physical damage you should be able to perambulate as normal in a few minutes."

Mia realized that she did have some feeling in her lower body. She had assumed she was paralyzed, but now that fear was receding as she tested her extremities for movement. She sat up with effort, and smiled at Gizmo.

"I thought they got rid of all your weapons."

Gizmo glanced down at its breastplate. Mia considered it an odd gesture for a robot.

"I could not bring myself to get rid of them all. So I kept this one secret." Its head moved up to focus on Mia. "Was this incorrect of me?"

"Not from where I'm sitting, Gizmo. But how come you didn't tell me about it?"

"Well, it wouldn't be secret then, would it?"

Mia laughed. "No, I don't suppose it would." She could move her legs a little now and decided she might try and stand. She held her hand out to Gizmo. "Help me up, will you?"

It took Mia a while to regain enough feeling in her battered body to walk unaided. But when she could, they made their way to a control center located at the back of the maintenance area. This was a large space filled with terminals and holo-tables used to manage the myriad of machines and processes that went on in the sector. It also had direct comms to Jezero City.

"Did you hear all that before you shot him, Gizmo?"

"I did."

"It's not a nuke, it's a bioweapon. We need to alert them. They have to ensure this terraforming event is canceled because it seems to be the trigger."

"I concur. Mia. This matches my own analysis of the situation." Gizmo switched on the holo-table and activated a comms link.

19

DECENNIAL CELEBRATIONS

Kane Butros, Second Director of the Mars Alliance Scientific Survey sat in the space station control room, which occupied one segment of the giant rotating torus. He was taking in the view of Mars afforded him by the wide observation window. The surface of the red planet slowly rotated counterclockwise, mirroring the speed and rotation of the observer's point of view. It also reflected the trajectory of the orbiting station as it circumnavigated the Martian poles. All this movement could be very disconcerting to the uninitiated, but after a while, most crewmembers got used to it and ceased to regard themselves as the object that was moving.

The station had just moved across Jezero Crater and was now tracking slowly over the vast Utopia Planitia as it headed for yet another pass over the North Pole. This would be the final pass before the thermonuclear detonation for the terraforming experiment finally occurred. But the event had been canceled and Kane Butros was not happy. Not because of any loss of scientific data but because the carefully laid plans of those that had put their faith in him to deliver, were now falling apart. It didn't help that Blake Derringer had gone offline, and could not be raised on comms for an update on his mission.

But Kane did not need a mystic to know that he was probably dead, since the powers that be in Jezero City now knew that a bioweapon had been hidden in their citadel, timed to detonate in tandem with the terraforming event. Worse, Evon Dent, the highest-ranking MASS director, was currently down on the planet starting up a thorough investigation.

All this was a major concern for Kane Butros. Nevertheless, he was not the type of person to lie down at the first hurdle. The situation, as he saw it, was compromised—this much was true. But he did have a plan B, and now was the time to set it in motion. He fished out his slate from a pocket, entered an eight digit alphanumeric code, and hit the INITIATE icon. Then he sat back and waited, it wouldn't take long.

And it didn't. Less than four minutes later three armed associates entered the control room of the MASS space station, to the astonishment of the assembled technicians.

"What the hell?" One foolhardy tech jumped up and objected to the carrying of weapons inside the control room. He was blasted. Fortunately non-lethal, merely stunned. But it did serve to underscore their intent. The rest of the techs turned to Kane, who rose from his seat.

"My apologies, but we are taking over this space station. You will now be escorted to a safe place, while we continue with our... eh, operation."

"Have you gone mad?" Another of the techs was beginning to sound like he might also be trouble, he too was blasted. Kane turned to his armed crew. "Try not to damage any of the control systems with those PEP weapons."

A crewmember nodded in reply. Several others entered and took up the positions vacated by the techs, and proceeded to reinitiate the terraforming event. After a moment or two the countdown on the main screen reset itself.

"The experiment has been reinstated, sir," a tech announced. The timer counted down—one hour and forty-six minutes to detonation.

"Excellent, replied Kane. He sat back down in the command chair and afforded himself a brief smile. *It's always good to have a plan B,* he thought.

∼

DR. JANN MALBEC paced up and down the operations room in Jezero City. On the main screen a feed was being relayed from a viewpoint overlooking the Avenue. The area was thronged with citizens as well as many of the contractors working for both the colony and the asteroid mining company, AsterX.

"Dr. Malbec, stop worrying." Evon Dent, the MASS chief operations officer tried to soothe Jann's growing unease. "The event has been canceled. And we will find this... device, wherever they've managed to hide it. It will be found."

Jann stopped pacing and looked down the Avenue to the stage and the screen behind it. It displayed an orbital view of Mars, a direct feed from the MASS space station. The countdown timer had been frozen. Initially there had been a general groan of disappointment from the crowd when the news broke that the terraforming event would not be taking place for the grand finale due to technical difficulties. But as more of the citizens' spirits were lubricated by the enormous quantities of beer and cider being dispatched from the Red Rock, the mood had grown steadily merrier.

On stage, Xenon Hybrid was recounting tales of his travels, and the rotating backdrop of the planet's surface married well with his dialogue. He had the full attention of the crowd by virtue of his oration and because this was the first time that many of the assembled had laid eyes on their enigmatic president.

But none of the throng knew the true situation, bar those with Jann in the operations room, and the crew that Nills had put together to sweep the facility to try and find the device. Evon Dent and his assistant had chosen to remain in Jezero City for the duration of the celebrations, rather than return to the space station as previously planned. But while this was a genuine gesture of solidarity it did little to allay fears over the plot to detonate a nuclear device in the city.

Jann's slate vibrated in her pocket, she fished it out. It was Mia. She tapped an icon to bring it up on the main screen so the others could see and hear. Mia looked bruised and battered. "It's not a nuke, it's a bioweapon. I don't know where, but its detonation is synchronized with the terraforming event."

"We've canceled the event," Evon said, as if he was letting Mia in on a big secret. Jann wasn't sure if Mia even heard him as she was rubbing her forehead and pushing back her hair.

"Where are you?" said Jann.

Mia looked around. "In the maintenance yard. The place is deserted, no one here. Just me and Gizmo. We're checking if any of the rovers here are working and then try to make it to Jezero City."

"What about that guy chasing you?" said Jann.

"Dead. That's all the information I could get out of him before Gizmo barbecued him."

"Okay, stay safe." Jann signed off.

"That robot is a danger to the colony, I cannot believe you let it loose armed with a plasma weapon." Yuto Yamashita was beginning to really piss Jann off.

"So you would prefer that Jezero City was annihilated?" Jann was pacing again.

"That's not the point. The threat, if there ever was one, is now under control. But a weaponized robot is still at large. I would say that's a problem," Yuto said with outrage.

"This is a totally irrelevant and pointless argument, Yuto. You're not helping. In fact, you're becoming a hindrance. So, can you please either shut up or get out," Nills snapped back.

But Yuto was not backing down, he was ready to fight when Evon raised a hand to get everyone's attention. He was looking at his slate, with a very concerned look on his face. "I think you all need to see this." He tapped the slate to bring the message up on the main monitor.

It was clearly a view from inside the orbiting space station. A MASS crewmember was taking a clandestine video from the control room. The image was blurred and shaky, but they could clearly see technicians being herded out by armed men. One was being dragged along the floor by the scruff of the neck, unconscious, maybe even dead. The camera swung around to show Kane Butros sitting in the command chair. Then the image shook wildly and the camera went dead.

Silence gripped the operations room in Jezero City for a moment as the implications of what they had just witnessed started to sink in. But before anyone spoke, they heard a loud cheer from the crowd down along the

Avenue. Nobody was sure what it was for until Jann realized the countdown clock for the terraforming event had been reset, and was running again.

"The timer, look." Jann pointed.

"Oh God," was the best that Evon could manage.

"Could someone please tell me what the hell is going on?" Yuto was clearly slower than the rest of them to fully realize what had just happened.

"Kane Butros has taken over the station, and restarted the event. We've got a little over an hour before…." Evon's sentence trailed off.

"Before what?" said Yuto.

"Before we're all dead," said Jann.

Nills was up on his feet. "We have to find it, whatever the hell it is. We have to find it and destroy it." He started contacting his search team. He had set up three separate teams equipped with Geiger counters, which were useless, now that the threat was no longer a nuclear weapon.

"The problem is we don't know what the hell we're looking for, what size it is, is it more than one device—this is impossible."

Jann knew things were serious when Nills started to use words like *impossible*.

"We have to evacuate." Yuto was also up on his feet. "Get everybody out now, before it's too late."

It was Jann's turn to use the 'I' word. "That's impossible, we don't have enough transport or EVA suits.

It would be bedlam, people could start to panic, it would be chaos."

"This is all your fault." Yuto was jabbing an accusatory finger at Jann.

Jann was resisting a very strong urge to eject the councilor from the nearest airlock when the operations room was plunged into darkness for a fraction of a second before the power came back on. There was another enormous cheer from down along the Avenue.

"What the hell was that?" said councilor Hoburg.

"Main power's gone down, we're on standby. " Nills spun around and started checking the control desks in the operations room. "Well that rules out evacuation. Now that we're on standby, all airlocks are sealed." He turned back to the group. "We'll have to cut our way out."

"Oh God, we're all gonna die," said Yuto.

Throughout all of this Evon had stared at the main screen and the hundreds of colonists gathered for the celebrations.

"Evon." Jann nudged him back to the here and now. "How are they doing this?"

He slowly turned to face her, shaking his head. "I don't know."

"Can you contact the station, talk to Kane Butros, find out what he wants?"

"I've tried, but comms are either dead or they're not responding."

"Goddammit, there must be a way to stop this," said Jann.

"There isn't. It's all automatically controlled from the station. The only way to stop it now would be to go up there and literally take back the station, it's just not possible. Unless..." he stopped and scratched his chin thoughtfully.

"What? Unless what?" shouted Jann.

"The antennae array. The devices are detonated by a transmission from the station. That needs the antennae to send the signal to surface. If that antennae were to be disabled then..."

"Well that's just crazy," said Robb. "And how the hell are we supposed to do that? Teleport up there?"

Evon was silent.

"Wait a minute, there might be a way." Jann turned back to Evon. "Your transport ship, the one you were going to use to return to the station before the event, it's still there, isn't it?"

Evon's eyes widened. "Yes, fully prepped, ready to launch."

"Then we can take it, get up there and knock out that antennae."

"Theoretically."

"We don't have time, Jann." Nills was shaking his head. "It will take a good twenty minutes to cut our way out, the same to get to the craft and then another forty between prepping and journey time. It's just not possible."

"And it can only hold four people, not enough to launch an armed takeover," Evon added.

"I'll go," said Yuto.

"Yeah, sure. Just so you can save your own ass," said Hoburg.

"There is a way," said Jann.

"How? Tell us," said Nills.

"Mia."

20

YOU WANT ME TO DO WHAT?

"You want me to do what?" Mia sat in the AsterX maintenance yard, listening with increasing incredulity, as Dr. Jann Malbec and Nills Langthorp explained to her, via a scratchy comms link, what they wanted her to do. Gizmo had gone off to survey the vehicles parked there to try and find one that worked, at least well enough to get them back to Jezero City. But now it looked like the plan was about to change.

"You have got to be kidding me!"

"You're the only one that can do it. Believe me, Mia, if there was any other way, we would try it, but we just don't have the time. The detonation is in less than an hour. We would barely get to the launch pad in that time." Jann's voice was pleading.

Mia shook her head. "But I have absolutely no idea

how to pilot a transport ship. I mean... seriously, this is crazy."

"You don't have to actually fly it." Nills added his voice to the conversation. "It flies itself autonomously. It will also rendezvous and dock on autopilot. You don't have to do anything."

"Oh really? What about the bit where I EVA and disable the antennae array?"

"Look, Mia." Jann took over again. "I know it's nuts. It's a totally insane plan. No one in their right mind would even contemplate such a high risk operation. But we have no other choice. I hate to lay this on you, Mia, but if you don't try this then we're all going to die—the entire population of Jezero City."

Mia stayed silent, arms folded, shaking her head.

"Mia." Jann's voice was softer now. "Will you do it?"

Mia lifted her head and looked back at the monitor. "I don't really have a choice, do I?" She stood up and shouted down into the maintenance area. "Gizmo, get your metal ass up here quick. You're really gonna love what they've planned for us this time."

ACCORDING TO NILLS, the plan was simple. According to Mia, it was insane, but that didn't matter anymore. She had put her mind to it, so it was either going to work or, as Jann so eloquently put it, they were all going to die. Already Gizmo had jacked into one of the terminals in the maintenance yard control room and was downloading launch codes from Nills over in Jezero. Once inside the MASS transport craft Gizmo would initiate the launch. From then on it would be automatic. All Mia had to do was sit back and enjoy the ride.

They had estimated it would take less than fifteen minutes to rendezvous with the orbiting space station, but Mia wouldn't be staying for the entire ride, and that was where the plan got interesting. She would EVA from the transport just before it docked. And with the help of a thruster jetpack, she would make her way down the central truss to the antennae array, where she would locate the main cable junction, and somehow disable it. And she had to accomplish all this within the next fifty-five minutes.

Gizmo jacked out of the terminal and spun around to Mia. "Ready?"

"As ready as I'll ever be. Come on, let's go."

Fortunately Mia's body had recovered somewhat. Gone was the numbness inflicted by the PEP blast. But her ribs hurt like hell, particularly when she breathed. And since she needed to do this to stay alive, there wasn't a lot she could do about the pain other than grin and bear it. She ran past the dismantled machines to the airlock where Gizmo had located a serviceable rover. It would take them to the MASS transport ship out at the spaceport, the very same place that Mia had touched down after her long trip from Earth. *Only six months ago,* she thought. *Now look at me.*

They clambered aboard and Gizmo wasted no time in

getting it started and prepped. They had begun to move toward the airlock when Gizmo stopped.

"What's wrong?"

"Comms from Jezero City, putting it on the main screen now." Nills' face materialized on the dash monitor.

"Are you still in the maintenance yard?"

"Yeah, just leaving now." said Mia.

"Well, hold off for a moment. I have something that might be of use. There's a strong room a short distance from the entrance. I'll send Gizmo a schematic with the exact location. Inside there should be a load of explosives that are used in the mines, along with remote detonators. Grab some and take them with you. They could be useful for disabling the array."

Mia checked the time. "This is cutting it tight."

"I know, it's your call, just thought I'd mention it."

Gizmo's head tilted around to Mia. "I calculate that acquiring the explosive devices will consume an additional three minutes and forty-seven seconds. It would be approximately eighty-three seconds less if I were to acquire them myself."

"Are you trying to put me out of a job, Gizmo?" Mia frowned at the droid. "Okay, go, go. I'll just wait here."

Gizmo charged off and left Mia to contemplate the enormity of the crime that was taking place. Who could even conceive of such a heinous act? To exterminate the entire colonist population on Mars. What demented reasoning could arrive at such a plan? Was it simply the madness of one individual? Mia doubted it. It had to be more than one psychopath let loose. There had to be more people involved. Even if everyone who had a hand in it didn't know the full extent of this madness, this genocide. And that's what it was, the extermination of an entire population of people. When she thought about it in those terms, she realized it was not so unique. How many times in human history was the fate of one group determined by the hate of another? Why? For what reason? But these questions were beyond Mia's reasoning.

Gizmo returned, carrying a box clearly labeled *explosives - danger*. It dropped it on the floor of the rover with such seeming carelessness it startled Mia.

"Should you not be more careful with those, Gizmo?"

"They are completely inert until primed. Perfectly safe." Gizmo moved into its position in the cockpit and started up the vehicle.

The rover bounced and rocked along the well worn road that wound its way to the spaceport at the very center of the crater. It seemed that all roads led here, this being the gateway to the trade and commerce of the colony. It had several landing and takeoff areas, depending on the size and type of craft. The largest pad was used for the big colony ships coming from Earth. These ships could accommodate a hundred people at a time. Huge, the size of a skyscraper, one of them was dominating the skyline as Mia and Gizmo made their approach. It had landed less than a week ago, carrying mainly tourists and officials that had arrived to partake in the decennial celebrations.

They swept past the foot of the great ship as they made their way to one of the ancillary pads. There were several of these dotted around the central apron. These facilitated the smaller ships, the ore freighters coming in from the asteroid belt, the Earth bound cargo vessels and transport ships that plied the route between the MASS and AsterX space stations. It was at one of these pads that Gizmo finally brought the rover to a shuddering, dusty halt.

Mia was already suited up and standing by the rear airlock when Gizmo hit the brakes to stop a few meters from the base of the craft. Mia exited the rover and made her way to a flimsy looking ladder running up one of the landing struts. From a distance the craft had looked small and fragile, particularly since she was comparing it to the behemoth that transported colonists from Earth. But now that she was up close and personal, it was considerably bigger than she had imagined. This gave her a little bit more confidence in the craft's ability to actually do the job of getting them to the space station. She started climbing.

The cockpit was not designed to accommodate a G2 unit, so Gizmo wedged itself in awkwardly between two seats just behind Mia, who was strapping herself down. Gizmo started talking her through the ignition sequence, which mostly involved bypassing all pre-launch safety checks. Flight controls were mercifully simple, consisting of a large main screen and a small tablet type pad on the armrest of each of the pilot seats. Mia punched in the codes Gizmo gave her and was furiously bypassing and muting all the alerts. Then there was a pause as the craft made contact with systems control on the space station orbiting above. The two systems would communicate autonomously, bypassing any requirement for human intervention. Delta V would be calculated along with a myriad of vectors to establish the correct launch trajectory for intercept with the space station and dock. But even though this was theoretically a computer-to-computer communication, its initiation would flash up on some technician's monitor onboard the space station. How would they react? Would it be allowed to lift off? And if so, would they be allowed to dock?

Nills, who seemed to know the most about these things, assured her that this interaction would happen so fast that there would be no time for the techs on the station to stop the launch. He neglected to mention what would happen in the intervening twelve minutes it took the craft to reach it. By then they might have guessed something was up and simply allow the craft to sail by, out into deep space. If that was the case, then Mia could be embarking on a very long journey indeed—that is, until her oxygen ran out.

After a few tense moments the armrest screen prompted Mia to enter the final launch code, then she hit the big blinking INITIATE button. Nothing happened, at least not that Mia could tell. But then she began to feel a slight vibration in her seat. It began to build in intensity to a point where Mia was gripping the armrests in a vain attempt to steady herself. When the full engine ignition finally came, it did so with such force that Mia felt she had been trapped in the jaws of a car crusher. Her cracked ribs had hurt before, now the pain was so intense she was at risk of passing out. And the noise was deafening, a violent cacophonous rage boiled all around her as the craft was propelled skyward.

Thankfully, it was short lived. When the noise and vibration finally stopped Mia found herself on the verge of unconsciousness. She tried hard to focus and bring her body back from the brink. All around her field of vision items were floating in the cockpit. They had broken free of Mars's feeble gravity and were weightless. Mia thought she heard a voice, or was it voices? Her hearing was shot.

"Mia... MIA..." Gizmo's bleatings finally made contact with her aural cavity.

"What...?"

"It is time for you to leave the capsule, if you dare."

The craft had no windows, but the main monitor acted as a virtual window out into space. In the frame Mia could see the enormous MASS space station dominating the view. They were coming in directly underneath it, heading for a docking port on the near end of the long central truss. The massive torus was too big to fit in the frame, but Mia could see a section of each of its four spokes gently rotate.

"Can we wait until we get closer?"

"A little. They have seen us coming and taken control of the craft. They are remotely decelerating us, preventing us from getting too close."

"Can't you hack it or something?'

"No, this capsule has no interface for a G2 unit so I can not interact directly with the systems. At best I could maneuver it using the orientation thrusters, but alas, we have no flight control. So I am powerless to do anything."

Mia sighed. The station looked a long way away meaning there was a high probability that she would sail right past it and out into deep space. But this was what she had come here to do, so she unstrapped herself and pulled herself to the airlock at the nose of the craft. It took a few moments for it to depressurize before the outer door finally opened and she glided out—into open space.

Mia's heart skipped a beat as she beheld the infinite expanse before her. Nothing she had ever seen or done at any time in her life had prepared her for the sheer exhilaration she experienced at that moment. It was like being born again, pushed out from the limitations and confines of the physical world and into the awe-inspiring vastness of the heavens.

"Mia, get ready." Gizmo's voice crackled in her headset and snapped her back to the reality of the situation. The plan was for her to take up a position on the outer shell of the craft as it slowed. Gizmo would signal her when to use her EVA suit thrusters to separate herself from the craft. She had absolutely no training in this other than a quick explanation from Gizmo on the short journey here. It was all theory, and the only thing she really picked up was that it was incredibly difficult to judge, as every action would propel her in the opposite direction—forever, until she compensated with an opposite action. So, from where she was standing right now, she was going to be learning on the job.

The space station was getting a little closer. *It must be nearly time*, she thought.

"Now," Gizmo signaled. Mia touched the controls, and found herself moving away from the transport craft. She resisted the temptation to fire her thrusters again. A little went a long way out here. For a while both Mia and the transport craft seemed to move in tandem, but as its momentum began to slow Mia found herself inching ahead.

Her initial fear of missing the station completely began to abate as she could see that she was on a good trajectory. She breathed a sigh of relief when she sailed over the docking dome in the nose of the station. *So far so good*. Then she realized she was also moving upward relative to the station, away from the central truss. That was okay for the moment, as she needed to get past the slowly rotating spokes of the giant torus. If one of those were to hit her on the way through, she would be knocked off course, out into deep space. Her thruster pack did not have the power to compensate for the additional momentum. But the higher she got the more of a gap there would be, so she maintained her focus.

Beyond the spokes, the long central truss thrust out into the distance. She could see the antennae array now, its large dish pointing straight at her, and down towards the planet's surface.

A spoke swept in front of her. From a distance they had seemed spindly and insubstantial. But up close they were as wide as a bus and probably carried as much momentum. She focused on the next spoke as it rotated towards her. Now that she was heading into its path it seemed to have picked up speed and was racing around faster than she liked. Again Mia resisted the temptation to fire her thrusters. Perhaps if she knew what she was doing she wouldn't be so panicked. But as she moved further into the track of the spoke she realized she was heading for impact. Mia hit the thrusters and accelerated forward just in time to sense the spoke pass safely behind her. But now she was moving way too fast. Her last thrust had also introduced a new rotational vector; she was spinning head over heels. *Goddammit.* She was losing her sense of position in space. *Where is up, where is down?* She had done the one thing she really didn't want to do—she had lost control. The universe outside her visor spun without reason. Mia calmed herself down and tried to make sense of her chaotic momentum. She focused on what she could see flying past her field of vision. After a few seconds she had determined one axis of rotation and fired her thruster pack to compensate; her spinning slowed. She did the same for another axis and finally managed to stop her rotation. But she was still moving away from the space station, not towards it, and she was fast running out of time. Mia fired her thrusters again and aimed for the antennae array. Now she came in too fast, missed the array, and bounced off the central truss. She scrambled furiously to grab on to something, anything. *Dammit.* She hit the thruster controls again and this time managed to wedge herself between two of the structural members of the truss. It wasn't very elegant but it was effective.

Mia stopped moving and tried to slow her breathing. It didn't help that her ribs had taken a battering bouncing off the station and responded with searing pain all around her upper chest. She groaned in agony. *Move. S*he forced her body to respond and extracted herself from the superstructure and onto the outside of the truss. She found that some thoughtful engineer had seen fit to populate one of the structural elements with handholds. She inched her way forward. The antennae assembly was much bigger and a lot more complex than it looked in the images she had studied on the journey up. But after a few moments, Mia could see where all the cables entered the structure. She took one of the explosive charges out of a pouch on the front of her EVA suit, activated it and wedged it in behind a bend in the cabling. She did the same with a second one. Now all she had to do was get far enough away that she could safely detonate it. She started to make her way back along the backbone of the space station, as fast as she could without losing her grip on it. After a few meters she began to wonder how far was far enough? Nobody had told her, or if they had, she had forgotten. She checked the time and found that she still had at least twenty-one minutes before the detonation of the terraforming event, and the bioweapon that had been hidden in Jezero City. So she decided to keep going further along the truss, that way she could leave plenty of room for error.

After a few moments of clambering along she arrived at the point where the massive torus connected with the backbone of the station. It rotated around a central axle about fifteen meters in diameter. This section, like the truss, did not rotate, it was fixed. Mia also noticed it had an airlock, presumably for maintenance crew to exit the station and conduct checks or repairs.

Mia moved around the truss to the underside, away from the antennae. She reasoned it might afford her better protection from any flying debris when she blew the array. She made sure she had a good grip on the truss before reaching into the front pouch on her EVA suit and withdrawing the detonator. This was a small black box with a short whip antennae. She opened the red cover and flicked the switch to charge the unit. A few tense seconds passed before a red LED lit up, indicating it was ready. *Okay,* she said to herself, *this is it.*

She turned the device over, slid open the cover on the detonate button, and realized to her horror that her gloved finger would not fit into the opening. *I don't believe it,* she said out loud.

"What?" came a reply in her headset, it was Gizmo on comm.

"Gizmo?"

"It is I."

"I can't activate the charges, my goddamn glove won't fit through the hole in the detonator."

"Oh dear, this is a problem we had not foreseen. Standard EVA suits used on the surface have much smaller gloves than these bulky spacesuits."

"You don't say," said Mia as she pressed harder, with no luck. Then she looked around on her EVA suit for some suitably sized prong that she could use instead. There was nothing. Presumably the designers had rightly figured that having things that stick out on an EVA suit could only get its occupant into trouble.

"Shit, shit. shit. I don't bloody believe this."

"Perhaps you could try and locate some suitable protuberance on the structure itself," offered Gizmo.

Mia was just about to do this when she noticed a light emanating from the other side of the structure. She pulled herself around to investigate. It was the airlock. The outer door was open and a figure floated out. It was checking, looking around. Mia ducked back down. It moved off down along the central truss.

"Gizmo," she whispered, not that she really needed to, as there was no way she could be heard in the vacuum of space, even if she screamed her head off.

"Yes?"

"The airlock just opened, I'm going inside." With that

she cautiously moved out from her concealed position. The suited figure was further down the central truss, so Mia clambered into the airlock, and hit the close button. The figure had noticed the movement and was zooming back down to try and get to her before the door closed. Too late. The door shut and the airlock began to pressurize. Mia waited until the green alert flashed then she flipped open her visor, powered down her suit and unclipped the glove from her right hand.

She removed the detonator from the pouch again, and was about to hit the button when the inner door of the airlock slid open with a sudden swoosh. Mia looked up in shock, as she recognized the person floating there aiming a PEP weapon directly at her.

"Christian?"

"Mia?" He fired.

Brilliant blue light burned into her retinas like a swarm of stinging insects. Her entire body was racked with pain as every muscle spasmed uncontrollably. Mia endured it for a few seconds before passing out.

21

SPACE STATION

Mia awoke from a slap across her face. She groaned, shook her head and blinked her eyes open. A blurred figure hovered over her and slowly came into focus. Mia recognized him. It was Christian. She spat out a gob of blood on the floor beside him.

As her senses returned Mia began to take stock of her surroundings. Across from her a tall person stood silhouetted against a panoramic window which framed a slowly rotating view of the planet Mars. His hands were clasped behind his back as he gazed out at the splendor of the vista. He turned around.

"Ah, Miss Sorelli, you are awake I see. I am Kane Butros." He paused to gesture at Christian. "And I believe you two have met before. You must have made quite an impression as your ex-boyfriend wanted to shove you out the nearest airlock until I intervened.

Mia didn't answer. Instead she leaned over and spat another gob of blood on the floor.

"Charming," came the reply as Kane approached her.

She realized then that she must be somewhere along the outer rim of the rotating torus, and the reason she found it difficult to move was because she was experiencing an extremely debilitating one gravity. Her body had gotten used to the one-third gravity on Mars and now struggled to deal with three times that. What made matters worse was that she was still encased in a very heavy EVA suit. Mia tried to move again but the best she could manage was a very inelegant rocking from side to side.

Kane came closer, pushing Christian aside, and held up the detonator that Mia had so desperately tried to activate in front of her face. "We can do this the easy way or the hard way. Where is it?"

Mia wasn't sure what the hell he was talking about but then realized that they had not found the explosives she had planted. That surprised her, as she really didn't try to hide them in any way. But maybe they thought she was trying to disable the station, or even destroy it, in which case they would not be looking anywhere near the antennae array. Perhaps they were searching the nuclear reactor or the main fuel tanks.

"I'll tell you what, I'll do a deal with you. You tell me where the bioweapon is hidden first."

Kane sighed. "Perhaps Christian is right. We should just shove you out an airlock without that suit and be done with you. Let's face it, it's not like you can do anything. Not without this, is there?" He waved the detonator at her again.

Mia managed to move her arm up to wipe some blood from her mouth, then let her head drop. "Go screw yourself."

Kane stepped back and looked down at her for a moment before redirecting his gaze to the surface of Mars. He gestured at the panorama. "Soon all this will end, and the debt will be paid."

Mia had no idea what the hell he was rambling on about, but she did realize that the terraforming event had not yet happened, so she still had time—at least, theoretically. But how much, she didn't know.

As her mind began to focus she could see a small group gathered around a holo-table, projecting a large 3D rendering of the planet. As it rotated, a myriad of data was displayed alongside, the most prominent of which was a countdown timer. It read four minutes and fifty-three seconds.

"Why?" Mia raised her voice as best she could to get Kane's attention.

He turned around and studied her.

"Why kill all those people, what do you hope to gain from this... genocide?" she continued.

"It seems you know very little of the history of this planet, Miss Sorelli." He paused for a moment before continuing.

"What you probably do know is, a decade ago a

highly virulent and destructive genetically engineered bacteria made its way back to Earth from Mars. It caused the deaths of millions, and spread panic around the world. This is common knowledge. But what most people don't realize is that the only person who knew how to kill it was your friend, Dr. Jann Malbec. However, she refused to reveal this knowledge to Earth unless Mars was granted independence. In doing so she caused more unnecessary deaths and suffering for a great many people. So you see Miss Sorelli, your sponsor has much blood on her hands."

"So that's it, that's what all this is about?" Mia waved a heavy arm around the control room. "An eye for an eye?"

"That, and the return of control of Mars to Earth."

"Ah... so there it is. Power and control, the favorite pastimes of the despot."

Kane spun around. "There are a great many on Earth who see things differently. Mars was stolen from us by Malbec and her cohort of clones. A great prize lost, the gateway to the riches of the asteroid belt. How much of human history is peppered with the rise and fall of the great city states, those whose power and wealth was gained by virtue of their geographical position on some lucrative trading route? Mars is no different, and Earth will soon regain control. When the terraforming event is triggered in a few minutes time, a deadly bio-toxin will be released into the environment of Jezero City, and everyone there will die. No more citizens. And with no citizens there can be no state, so control returns to the UN."

Mia remained silent as she frantically tried to think of something she could do to avert this catastrophe. Kane had returned his gaze to the window and the surface of Mars. "This has been a long time in the planning. For years we sought to infiltrate and influence both the council on Mars and the board of MASS. All that work and effort now comes to fruition." He turned back to Mia. "Not even your pathetic attempts or that witch Malbec can stop it now."

"What about the courier... the clone that died when his rover blew up?" An idea was forming in Mia's mind. It was probably futile, but she had to try something, so she kept him talking.

"What? Oh him. Well we needed someone with intimate knowledge of Jezero City to transport and hide the bioweapon. Who better than a clone? You know, they will do anything for the promise of a ticket back to Earth."

"He was never going back, was he? So you got rid of him?"

"There's no way we could have him go back to Earth, so yes. Blake Derringer did a nice job on that rover. Nobody would have found out, and I would not have had to reveal myself this early on, if it wasn't for your meddling."

While Kane Butros had been rambling on, Mia had booted up her suit. Not that she was planning to EVA, but she wanted the thruster pack activated. It was a desperate idea, because even though a little thrust went a long way in the weightlessness of space, how much she could move in one gravity was questionable. Nonetheless, Mia cranked the power up to max, aimed herself at Kane, and hit the button.

The initial burst lifted her to a standing position, but from then on she lost control and tumbled her way across the room, cartwheeling as she went. She whacked into Kane, sending him flying over the holo-table. The detonator fell out of his hand and rolled along the floor.

Mia cut the power to her suit thruster and flopped face down on the floor. Almost immediately she felt a heavy kick to her side but the suit took most of the sting out of it. She rolled onto her back to see Christian. He had a PEP in his hand ready to fire. "I should have thrown you out the airlock the first time."

Mia glared at him. "Go screw yourself." Only then did he realize she was holding the detonator. She hit the button.

She felt a slight tremor ripple through the station. The others in the room felt it too and they all turned to look out the window on the opposite side from the Martian vista. This looked out at the central truss. Mia sat up to get a better view. She could see the antennae array was completely destroyed. Debris was flying in a hundred different directions. The large dish had detached and was tumbling through space—straight at them. There was a brief moment of complete stillness in the control room while its occupants watched in horror as the speeding dish slammed into the window. The station rocked with the force of the impact. Everyone stood stock still, all eyes on the window, all waiting to see if it survived the collision. It didn't.

A crack appeared and everybody looked around frantically for the exits. Mia looked around for her helmet. It was over where she had first woken up. With everybody distracted by the potential loss of station integrity she scrambled her way back to it. Her glove was still attached by its umbilical so she clipped it on. But as she was about to grab the helmet a boot came down hard on her arm. "Where the hell do you think you're going?" It was Christian. He brought the muzzle of the PEP weapon right up to her face. "Time to die."

The window shattered.

The entire contents of the control room started being sucked out into the vacuum of space, including Christian. He fired the PEP weapon as he tumbled backward towards the gaping hole in the window. But his aim was random, the plasma blast crackling across the ceiling.

Mia could feel herself being pulled along. She still had the helmet but she struggled to attach it as she bounced and banged her way across the floor. Already she could hear the screams of technicians being sucked outside. She finally clipped the helmet on as the window gave way completely, and she, along with everyone else that was in the control room were vented out into space. Through her helmet visor she could see the body of Kane float past. Mia tried to shift her position to look for Christian, but she had no controls. The thruster pack was empty, having used up all its reserves in her bid to grab the detonator. She was drifting away from the station, out into deep space, with no way to stop, and no way to get back. She had halted the terraforming event and prevented the genocide. But with no control over her own momentum, she knew she was dead, it was simply a matter of time.

Mia lost all sense of motion and felt instead a strange sense of calm. The vast panoply of stars enveloped her and she began to experience a deep existential epiphany. She felt at one with the universe, compiled from the very atoms that had been forged in the celestial cauldron that expanded out all around her into infinity. At that moment Mia felt an inner peace so profound that she was content to die now, in this place, surrounded by the heavens.

She woke some time later to a staccato burst of static emanating from her helmet comms. She had been hearing it for quite some time but it had failed to penetrate her semi-unconscious state. Now though, she thought she heard voices somewhere in the depths of the white noise.

She had been floating out into deep space for quite a while. How long she wasn't sure. It was hard to gauge as she seemed to be drifting in and out of consciousness, or maybe that was an illusion. Her head was fuzzy and she had difficulty in making sense of her surroundings. More static burst out from her comms.

"Hello?" she ventured. Her voice was shallow, as if she had forgotten how to speak. She tried again. "Hello, anyone hear me?"

Silence, then another quick burst of white noise. This time Mia sensed it was trying to communicate with her.

"Hello? I'm still alive—I think." She waited for a reply, but as the moments passed and no more static emanated from her comms, she decided she had just been hallucinating.

Time passed and again she lost track of how much. There had been no more comms activity and she had resumed her resigned frame of mind. But something was changing—it was getting darker. *How is that possible? Am I dreaming?* No, she could see the stars in her peripheral vision being blocked out, one by one. She sensed something ominous sneaking up behind her. She shifted her head in her helmet to try to get a better view, but it was pointless. Nonetheless, there was no mistaking it, she was being slowly enveloped in a cone of darkness. It surrounded her, leaving only a small patch of stars ahead of her, and that too was growing smaller and smaller with each passing second. Mia felt as if she was being swallowed by some great spacefaring whale.

As the darkness finally engulfed her, she was bumped by something behind her, pushing her forward until she banged off something hard. She reached out to touch it and in the illumination reflected from her helmet she could see it was metal. *What is this?* But before Mia could answer her own question the lights came on and she realized she was in the airlock of the MASS transport craft that she and Gizmo used to take off from Mars. She felt it pressurize and saw the green light illuminate. It was with a deep sense of trepidation that she reached up to remove her helmet. Mia wasn't sure if this was really happening or if it was just an elaborate hallucination. She heard a slight hiss as she unfastened it, then she removed it completely and took a tentative breath.

The inner door opened and Mia twisted her body around, pushing herself into the capsule cockpit. Gizmo was at the controls. The little robot had managed to maneuver itself into a position that allowed it to access the flight controls. A rather awkward arrangement, as the transport craft's flight control was not designed with a G2 interface. It spun its head around as Mia entered, and waved a metal hand.

"Greetings, Mia."

"Gizmo, how the hell did you get here?"

"When the space station control room was destroyed, so too were the systems commandeering this craft. I was able to take command. I tracked your unorthodox evacuation from the station and calculated your exit vector and velocity. A quick analysis of the craft's flight capability, using only the very limited maneuvering thrusters, confirmed a 53.4% probability of retrieving you. Of course, I still had no data on the integrity of your EVA suit, so I had no way of ascertaining if you would be dead or alive when we rendezvoused."

The oxygen rich environment of the capsule was clearing Mia's head. She floated down into a seat and strapped herself in.

"Well, thank you, Gizmo. I had pretty much accepted that I would die out there." She took some time to take stock of her change of fortune. "So, where to now? I presume this craft can't land back down on Mars."

"Correct. However, we can return to the station and dock."

"But that's destroyed."

"Only partially. The control room is now open to the vacuum of space. But the rest of the facility is still intact."

"Okay, the station it is then."

22

STAR

Mia sat on the patio of her new accommodation pod in one of the recently completed housing domes. Although it was more of a cylinder than a dome, with three levels of accommodation pods built around an open tropical garden, and capped with a translucent domed roof. It was spacious compared to the one allotted to her on arrival nine months ago. This one could almost be considered an apartment by any standard.

It had been given to her as a perk of the new role she was about to take on, as director of the newly created local police force. This was being set up as a response to the need for better dispute resolution. It would also be an official point of contact for colonists who had been subjected to the normal run of the mill crap that most communities have to deal with when they get bigger. It was the kind of municipal agency that Mia could have engaged with when her ex-boyfriend ran off with her jewelry box. If it had existed back then, perhaps she wouldn't have had to take the drastic action she did. But then again, it would have been a different story, with a very different outcome.

In many respects Mia had failed in her primary mission. Sure, she saved the citizens of Mars from extermination, but she still had not retrieved her jewelry box. So, the case was still open, and as such, it would be number one on her list when she took up her new role. She sipped her tea as she sat and watched two small birds drink from the fountain in the center of the garden. Mia marveled at how they had adapted to flight in one-third gravity. With just a few flaps of their wings they could fly high into the dome superstructure where they kept their nests. To descend from these heights they seemed to just glide down on outstretched wings, like cormorants riding the thermals along cliff walls.

She still had some time to kill before the ceremony. They would be presenting her with an honor, recognition for her heroism in saving all their asses. Mia was not looking forward to it, in fact she was dreading it. It reminded her too much of times past, attending similar ceremonies back on Earth, where medals were pinned on the heroes or solemn words said for the fallen. But there was no denying she had earned her place among the pantheon of figures that had forged the colony into what it was today. Those who had protected it from both the inhospitable environment and the inhumanity of their fellow species. There was even talk of a statue in her likeness being erected alongside the titans of Martian history, Malbec, Xenon, and the others. But even though Mia was glad to have come through the ordeal with her life intact, deep down she felt as if she had not got full closure. There was a gap there, the mission was still not complete.

After Gizmo had navigated their way back to the damaged MASS space station and docked, they found that the main crew had regained control and were busy dealing with the aftermath of both the coup and the destruction that Mia had inflicted on the facility. Nonetheless, their craft was quickly refueled and Mia decided it would be best to hightail it out of there and back to Mars asap. She never got a chance to root through Christian's belongings to find her jewelry box. But in the weeks and months that followed, when the full facts of the planned genocide were revealed to the citizens, they became so incensed that repercussions were inevitable. MASS were evicted from Mars and herded onto an Earth bound transport. All their facilities, including the space station were commandeered by the council as reparations, much to the howls of protest that were now emanating from the UN back on Earth. Even the Mars council were not spared the wrath of the wronged. Those that had sided with MASS or even argued that MASS was also a victim were dealt with harshly. Justice would not only be done, but it would be seen to be done. And so a purge of sorts had begun and things could have gotten ugly if not for the fact that cooler heads had prevailed and established an equilibrium of sorts.

During this period Mia had kept her head down, even though she was the subject of much praise, bordering on adulation. She smiled, and nodded, and kept her mouth shut. She was acutely aware what it was like to be on the other side of the coin, when the world has turned against you. She knew it would all settle down after a time, and people would go back to worrying about the more mundane things in life, with MASS and their apologists ceasing to be headline news.

SOMETHING MUST HAVE STARTLED the two birds at the fountain as they flew off in unison, up to the safety of the superstructure. Mia followed their path upwards with her eyes, and then heard a familiar whirring sound. She looked around to see Dr. Jann Malbec walking towards her. The whirring sound was Gizmo following beside her. Mia stood up and waved as they approached.

"Is it time?" she said.

"Shortly. We still have a few minutes. I came a little early because I have something for you." Jann took a seat, Mia sat down opposite her, Gizmo whirred in beside them.

"Good to see you, Gizmo. It looks like you've had a few upgrades." Mia admired the new appendages the little droid sported.

"Thank you. It is good to see you too, Mia. And yes, I have had my full complement of weaponry restored." A compartment opened on one of the robot's shoulders and a plasma weapon extended outward. It swiveled around, pointing in different directions before retracting again.

"That looks very intimidating." Mia laughed.

"My thoughts exactly," said Gizmo.

"I have something for you, Mia." Jann reached in the folds of her robe and extracted a small wooden box, no bigger than a pack of cigarettes. It was old and battered and looked as if it had lived a long life. She handed it to Mia.

"I believe this is yours."

Mia hesitated for a second, not believing what she was seeing. Then she reached out and tentatively took the box, clasped it in both hands, and looked at Jann.

"Where did you get this?"

"We finally did a search of Christian Smithson's personal effects. This was in one of his bags, along with a number of other missing items."

"I don't believe it." Mia looked at her jewelry box, the one she had spent so much time and energy trying to get back. "I was beginning to think I would never see it again." She set it down on the table and opened the hinged lid all the way. Inside were some small items, earrings, a few bracelets, rings. At the bottom of the box was a piece of folded paper, which Mia extracted. She opened out the folds and a small, cheap pendant fell out onto her hand. She held it up for Jann to see. It was a small six sided star, cheaply made from thin pressed metal. At its center was a small red plastic gemstone. It looked like something a child might wear.

"This is what I risked my life to get back." She handed it to Jann, who took it and examined it.

"It must mean a lot to you."

Mia was reading the worn and tattered note that the pendant had been wrapped in. A tear came to her eye as she read it. She wiped it away, sat back and looked at Jann.

"You know, I never really believed you, that first time we met. I'll be honest, Jann. I thought you were just some crazy paranoid weirdo."

Jann laughed. "Well, you're not the only one. I think that may have been the general consensus at the time."

"You know, the only reason I took the job was to get back this note and that pendant you're holding. Your job offer was a way for me to go after Christian. I knew he must have taken it. I never, for one minute, considered you might have been right about the murder of that courier at Nili Fossae."

Jann didn't say anything for a moment. She was looking back and forth between Mia and the pendant.

"I know what you're thinking. I must be bonkers, it's

just a cheap kids toy. The type of thing you'd find in a Christmas cracker. And yes, on face value that's exactly what it is. But it's also what saved my life and brought me back from the brink."

Mia leaned forward. "Let me tell you a story, something I've never told anyone else before now. You know what happened to me, back on Earth, killing that kid and all the crap that got dumped on my head. It was all in that report you read. But what's not in the report is, about a year after, I was in a bad place, drinking, popping pills. I was a mess and my life was going down the toilet fast. Anyway, one morning after an all night binge I discovered to my horror I had drunk all my stash. So there was nothing for it except to leave my shithole apartment and score some more. I was so drunk it took me a while to stumble to the store. That's when things got really messy. I don't really know what happened exactly. But the owner called the cops and I was hauled off, kicking and screaming, at least that's what they said.

"I spent the night in a cell downtown and sobered up. The cops all knew who I was, of course, so they went easy on me. Next morning I got out and made my way home. When I got there someone had left a copy of the local rag nailed to my front door. The headline read, *Kid Killer Cop Arrested for Drug Store Hold Up.*" Mia sat back in her chair.

"It wasn't true, of course, at least not the hold up bit. But it was the last straw. Something in me cracked, I couldn't take any more. So I decided to end it all with a drug overdose. The only problem was it would take me a few days to score enough to do the job."

Mia picked up the letter and showed it to Jann. "Then two days later, before I had time to off myself, this came sliding in under my door."

Jann took the note and started reading it. She looked up at Mia when she finished.

"Yeah. And this was inside it." Mia held up the pendant.

"It was from the woman whose kid I'd killed. She had watched me being dragged through the courts and vilified in the news. She had witnessed my steady descent into an alcoholic drug addict. She had every reason to hate my guts and want me dead. But instead she sends me this note and a pendant that belonged to her little girl. You see, she forgave me. She didn't want me to be another victim in that awful tragedy. She had seen the headline in the paper a few days earlier and she reached out to help me. Can you imagine what it must take for someone to do that, Jann?"

Jann shook her head gently.

"I had taken away her little girl and yet she had it within her to try and help me. I could totally understand if she despised me. In my mind she had a right. Not like the others who simply hate for ratings, or worse, for entertainment. No, she had the right, and she chose not to." Mia stopped and brushed a tear from her eye. Then she held up the pendant again.

"She sent me this as a gesture, something to remind

me of her girl, a token to let me know that she held no malice for me." Mia went quiet for a while, just holding the pendant in her hand.

"Anyway, it's what saved me," she said after rubbing away a last tear. "I decided from that moment on I would clean up my act, get sober, put my life back together. I'm not saying it was easy, no. It was hard, but when times got tough I would take this out and hold it, and it would give me the strength to carry on."

Mia smiled at Jann. "So you see, there was no way I was going to let some two bit loser like Christian get away with stealing it. It just wasn't going to happen. I would have hunted him down until the end of time. That's why I took you up on the job offer. It was a way for me to go after him and get it back. Even if that meant I would have to blow up the MASS space station and prevent the genocide of the colony in the process, then so be it."

The two women sat in silence for a while before Jann reached over and picked up the pendant again. She studied it for a moment, this time in a new light, before she finally spoke. "Tell me, have you ever worn it?"

Mia shook her head. "No... I couldn't."

"Why not."

"I never felt worthy, I suppose."

Jann handed it back. "I see no reason that a symbol of all that is good about humanity should not be on display."

Mia looked at the pendant for a few moments, contemplating it. Then she undid the clasp on the chain and hung it around her neck. She sighed as she pressed her fingers to the star now hanging around her neck. "Okay, Jann. I'm ready now."

THE END

Why not check out my new series, The Belt.

Extract from the First Book of Martian Poetry, by Xenon Hybrid, President of Mars. As recited at the decennial celebrations.

The Plains of Utopia
Dust devils dance
Twisting and entwining
Like an alien ballet
Dusty vortices track the surface
As I reach out to touch
And move as they do
To be as one
With the spirits of Mars
Far out, on the Plains of Utopia

Reproduced by kind permission of the Government of Mars and The Greater Martian Territories.

ALSO BY GERALD M. KILBY

You can also find the next book in the series, Surface Tension: Colony Five Mars, here.

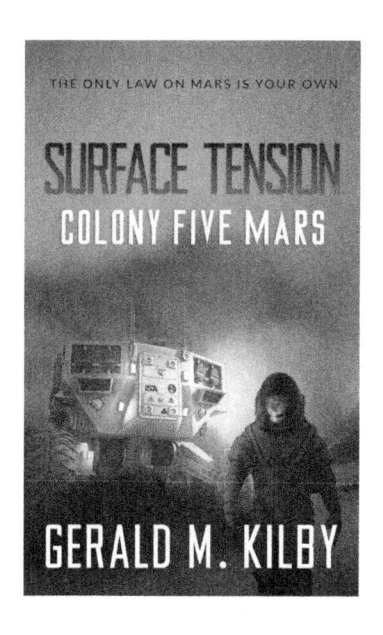

In the midst of the most devastating dust storm in the history of Mars, the survival of the half million people who call it home is hanging in the balance.

ABOUT THE AUTHOR

Gerald M. Kilby grew up on a diet of Isaac Asimov, Arthur C. Clark, and Frank Herbert, which developed into a taste for Iain M. Banks and everything ever written by Neal Stephenson. Understandable then, that he should choose science fiction as his weapon of choice when entering the fray of storytelling.

REACTION is his first novel and is very much in the old-school techno-thriller style and you can get it free here. His latest books, **COLONY MARS** and **THE BELT,** are both best sellers, topping Amazon charts for Hard Science Fiction and Space Exploration.

He lives in the city of Dublin, Ireland, in the same neighborhood as Bram Stoker and can be sometimes seen tapping away on a laptop in the local cafe with his dog Loki.

Printed in Dunstable, United Kingdom